RENEWED

The Unexpected Series

S.E. ROBERTS

s.e. roberts

renewed

the unexpected series
book two

Renewed

The Unexpected Series: Book Two

Copyright © 2019 by S.E. Roberts

All rights reserved.

Formatting by: Jessica Ames

Cover design by: Lauren Dawes at Sly Fox Cover Designs

Edited by: Sara Miller at Pretty Little Book Promotion

Edited by: Trenda London at It's Your Story Content Editing

Proofread by: Dominque Laura at Dom's Proofreading

To my wonderful husband who makes me laugh every single day. I couldn't do this crazy life without you. I love you.

AVERY

I wake with a start when the alarm on my phone starts blaring loudly beside me. I really, *really* don't want to go to work today. The fact that we have our four-month sonogram this afternoon is the only thing that is going to get me through the day. At our last appointment, we were told that as long as the baby cooperates, we will get to find out the gender today. I had thought I wanted to wait, but Evan talked me into it. He said that he was leaving work at lunch for the day so we can go shopping for the baby once we're done at the appointment. I've had several people ask me if I want a boy or girl, but honestly, I just want a healthy baby. I'd love seeing my husband playing with a little boy, but at the same time, he'd make an awesome father to a girl because he's so overprotective. Although, God help her, she won't be getting married until she's forty. Either way, our child is going to be loved.

I rub at my eyes as I prop myself up on my pillow that rests against the headboard, then grab my phone to flip through Facebook before I hop in the shower. I don't hear the shower going, so Evan must have left earlier than normal. I'm so lost in thought as I mindlessly scroll through my phone that I don't hear him enter our bedroom.

"Hey, beautiful," I nearly jump off the bed in surprise. "Sorry, didn't mean to scare you." He smirks. "Hungry?" He walks to my side of the bed and sets down a plate of eggs, bacon, and toast, and then a bowl of fruit on the nightstand.

"Oh, my goodness, babe. This looks amazing." I yawn and raise my arms above my head in a stretch and then lean my head back to kiss him as he bends down to my level. When I pull back, I ask, "Aren't you going to be late for work? I thought you were already gone."

"I ended up not having to go to Scottsdale, so I didn't have to leave as early." My handsome husband joins me on the other side of the bed. He's dressed in a navy blue, pinstriped suit with a baby blue shirt peeking out the top. The tie around his neck is white with light blue stripes. He's gorgeous. I almost don't want to let him out of the house looking this good. I know that any woman who sees him will be drooling. I really can't blame them though.

I scoop a spoonful of eggs onto my toast and then take a bite.

"Well, you, Mr. Porter, look good enough to eat." I wink at him and then turn back to my food.

"Mrs. Porter, if you want to make it to work on time, you better not say things like that to me." He raises his eyebrows at me.

"What if I don't want to go to work?" I waggle my eyebrows and then purposely pull my shirt down so he can see the tops of my breasts, and I'm aware that he's watching my every move.

He sets his nearly empty plate and his coffee mug on the table next to him and then takes mine from my hands.

"Hey! I wasn't done with that."

In the next instant, I'm underneath him.

At first, he doesn't say anything but breathes heavy as he searches my eyes.

"Oh, fuck it." He climbs off of me, and I wonder what he's doing until he starts loosening his tie, and then the rest of his clothes come off. The tattoos on both his arms make him even more delicious. The right one is covered with a beautiful rose, outlined in black with red shaded throughout. His mom loved roses. It's beautiful and completely masculine. The other arm has a four-leaf clover the size of my fist, with our anniversary date in the middle. He always says my eyes are the color of clovers. I get the best of both worlds. My man is sexy as hell in a suit, but underneath he is just as nice to look at.

"What are you doing?" I have to cross my legs because of the ache that is about to erupt between them. Just the sight of him acting like this is making me ridiculously wet.

He walks back toward the bed and then lifts me so my legs automatically wrap around his body.

"My wife is very dirty and needs a shower." He carries me to the bathroom.

"Babe, you already showered. Aren't you worried you'll be late?" I hope to God that he doesn't change his mind, but I really don't want him to get in trouble.

"Well, then I guess we better hurry."

He sets me on the counter and strips my clothes off in

record time. When my panties are off, he lifts them to his nose and inhales my scent, and I about orgasm just from the sight. Holy. Fuck.

"Damn, Av. You smell fucking delicious. You're ready for me, aren't you?"

Oh, dear God. There's no way I'm going to last long. Instead of answering him with words, I bite down on my bottom lip. I don't think I could form a coherent sentence right now if I had to.

He rests both his hands on either side of my ass and then stares at me for a brief moment before consuming my mouth with his. It ends quicker than I'd like when he leaves me to start the shower.

He lifts me off the counter, and my legs wrap around him, and I instantly feel his hardness poking my stomach. I have a feeling he isn't going to last long either. I guess that's a good thing since we both have to get to work, but I want more than anything to spend the day wrapped around this naked man.

Once we're in the shower, me still in his arms, he pushes me against the wall and starts fucking my mouth with his tongue. He pulls back from my mouth but then runs his tongue along my bottom lip and then lightly bites down. The small action has me almost coming completely undone in his arms.

"You want me to fuck you, baby?" He rasps out. This is obviously affecting him as much as it is me.

"Yes." I barely get the word out before he's pounding into me, causing me to scream. He carries me to the bench in the corner of the shower and sits down. I then have better control and start to bounce up and down on his rock-hard cock.

He reaches between us and flicks once at my clit, and I shatter to pieces while sitting on him. Everything around us starts to spin, and I'm pretty sure I see stars.

Evan explodes inside of me seconds later, his warm seed filling me. I throw my head back and grip at his hair as we both come down from our highs.

"God, I fucking love you." He gives me a sweet kiss, which is complete opposite of what we just did to each other.

When the kiss ends, I smirk at him. "I fucking love you, too."

"Hi, what can I help you with?" the young blonde behind the counter asks.

"I'm Avery Porter. I have a one o'clock appointment with Dr. Cooper."

After checking in, I make my way to the chair next to Evan. He's got a magazine in his hand that he's flipping through, and then I realize that it's a parenting magazine. He quickly puts it on the table beside him when he sees that I noticed.

"Pick that back up, babe." I smile at him.

He leans over the armrest to kiss me, but we're interrupted when a nurse calls my name.

The young nurse, who is also pregnant, weighs me and then hands me a gown and tells me the doctor will be in shortly. I'm suddenly nervous to see my baby on the screen again. It sounds silly because this isn't our first sonogram, but I always worry that something could possibly be wrong.

"Well, Avery, let's see if this little one will let us see what he or she is." Dr. Cooper gives me a small smile and then pages his sonographer to our room.

After what seems like forever, a short petite woman with dark hair pushes a cart into the room. I learn that her name is Celeste. The cart holds a computer where my baby will appear on the screen shortly. She rubs the ice-cold gel on my stomach and then rolls the wand around, trying to find the little nugget. We're all silent but then hear the *whoosh whoosh* sound that comes from the monitor. It's hard to believe that it's our child, after struggling with infertility for so long. The little one is only the size of an avocado right now, their words, not mine, but we are still able to tell that it's a baby.

"The heartbeat sounds great. Are you wanting to find out the gender today?" Celeste asks us both without removing her eyes from the screen.

"Yes, please." We both answer at the same time. Evan grabs my hand in a tight grip, obviously excited about what we're going to find out.

I impatiently lay on the bed. When Celeste doesn't say anything, I look up at my husband to see that he's staring at the screen as if it may disappear if he takes his eyes off of it.

"There she is!" She shrieks. *She.*

"It's a girl?" I croak out and feel a tear slide down my face. I'm having a little girl.

"Yes! Congratulations!"

She clicks on a few more things to get pictures and then shuts down the computer.

"I'm going to go print these pictures out for you, but I'll be right back."

Once she is gone from the room, I take a look at Evan. He's staring into space.

"What do you think, babe?" I whisper up at him.

He finally turns to look at me. "I'm fucking excited." He smiles and then gives me a breathtaking kiss. "This little girl is going to be so damn loved." He rubs at my stomach and then leans down to kiss it, not caring that it still has gel on it.

❧ 2 ❧

EVAN

It's been a week since we had Avery's appointment and found out that we're having a girl. It still seems unreal. I know that she's excited as she's already picked out furniture and bedding for the nursery. We are now on our way to pick out paint. After much research, we found a store that sells odorless paint, so it's safe for both Avery and the baby. She, of course, insisted that she help, because what kind of interior designer would she be if she didn't design her own child's nursery? My wife is stubborn as a mule, but I have learned that arguing with a pregnant woman definitely gets me nowhere.

"What about Luna?" she asks from the passenger seat. She's found a baby name website, and we've been discussing names for the last several days. Not agreeing on anything so far.

"As in the moon?" I chuckle but then quickly shut up once I realize she's completely serious. "Av, that's beautiful, but what else you got?" I give her hand a quick squeeze but then release it so I can go back to driving in the crazy Phoenix traffic.

She pouts. "You don't like anything I suggest." She huffs and then goes back to looking at her phone. "Liliana, Logan, Lucia...." I see her look at me out of the corner of my eye. "I don't know. What the hell do you like?"

"Logan? Isn't that a boy name?"

"Gender neutral names are the thing now." She throws her phone in her purse and then crosses her arms across her gorgeous tits as she throws herself back in her seat.

"I just want our princess to have the perfect name." I wink at her.

"Seriously? At this rate, this child won't have a name when she comes out." I know there's no use arguing. If you've never been around a pregnant woman, take note. You will lose, even if you're right. Oh, and never tell your pregnant wife that you're right.

"What about Anna or Erica?" I ask as we pull into the parking lot at the paint store.

"So, you like boring names?" She raises her eyebrows at me. "Okay, they aren't boring, but come on, babe. Our daughter needs something unique."

"Okay, so you'd rather give her a boy's name instead?" Shit. That was not the smartest thing to say.

"Oh, my God! You're impossible!" She throws her door open, nearly hitting the car next to us, and storms into the store. Not caring that I'm still sitting in the Jeep. Shit.

I finally grow a pair and follow my wife into the store and find her looking at different shades of purple on a paint swatch.

"Hey gorgeous, what did you find?" I ask, hoping and

praying that she's already over our baby name conversation.

"Do you like mulberry?" She shows me a deep purple color, "or something lighter like lilac or opal?" She shows me two more colors, which, honest to God, look identical to me.

I take them from her and hold each up toward the light.

We decide on lilac paint. I'm a dude and could care less, but I need to appease my wife. Next, she picks out paint for the baseboards, and then we're on our way home.

"I talked to Claire today, and she suggested that we register for Lamaze classes soon," Avery says as we pull into the garage. I grab the paint out of the back seat, and we head inside.

"What classes?" I have no idea what the hell she's talking about.

"Lamaze. It's where they teach you different breathing techniques for when you're in labor."

"And this actually helps? If I recall correctly, Ryke told me that my sister acted like she was possessed while she was in labor with Aria." I laugh.

"He actually said that?" She laughs as she rolls her eyes. "No wonder she threatened to snip him herself if she gets pregnant again."

After I set the paint inside the nursery, I pull her into my arms.

"You women are evil," I mumble into her hair. "You're not going to do that to me, are you?"

She snickers. "I don't know. Do you think you're going

to keep knocking me up after this one?" She looks up at me with mischief in her eyes.

I honestly hadn't put much thought into it. After all the struggles we had to get pregnant this time, I never really imagined that we'd have more than one. When I don't answer her right away, she looks at me with concern on her face.

She grabs my face with both her hands. "Ev, what's wrong? If you want more, just give me a couple years, okay?" She kisses my nose.

"Nothing is wrong. I just never really thought we'd have more after this one." I rub at her still small stomach that is pressed against me.

"Well, who knows what will happen? We'll at least have this little princess to spoil." I nod at her, and then she kisses my cheek before walking toward the kitchen to start dinner.

"HEY, BIG BRO," my sister says as she comes through the front door and pulls me into a hug.

"Hey, thanks for helping Avery with the nursery." I had offered to help, but the girls wanted to do it, so who was I to argue?

"No problem. Any excuse to get time away from the kids." She winks and heads toward the kitchen where my wife is.

Me and Ryke follow behind, and I pull two beers out for us, and then we tell the girls we're going to hang out in the living room until dinner is ready.

We have dinner consisting of twice baked potatoes

and salad, and then Avery goes to change into different clothes before they start to paint.

I'm lost in conversation with Ryke and Claire that I don't notice right away when she exits our room.

Holy. Shit. How is it that my wife is so damn beautiful all the time? She could be wearing a paper bag over her head and I know that I'd still find her sexy as hell.

She absentmindedly wiggles her ass as she makes her way toward me and then sits on my lap as I sit in the recliner, my sister and Ryke across from us.

It's taking every fucking ounce of my control to keep from stripping her damn clothes off her. She's wearing cut-off jean shorts that are making my cock hard under her ass, with a lime green tank top. Her pregnant belly is peeking out the bottom, and maybe it's weird, but it's a damn turn on.

She turns around and looks at me in shock, clearly feeling me poking her. I know I should be embarrassed, but I really can't bring myself to care.

"Seriously, Ev?" She shakes her head at me.

I chuckle at her. "Avery Porter, if you didn't wear shit like this around my house, I wouldn't have such a hard time keeping my dick in my pants," I whisper this to her as Claire and Ryke are wrapped up in their own conversation across the room.

"You're ridiculous." She giggles and then gets off my lap and makes her way to the nursery with Claire. I grab the blanket off the back of the chair to cover my lap, willing my hard-on to disappear.

❧ 3 ❧

AVERY

My work day is finally over, and I'm exhausted. It's truly a miracle that I stayed awake long enough to get anything done today. My best friend from work, Carly, kept asking me if I was alright, and I kept nodding as I yawned.

"I'm in the living room!" Sierra hollers from the other side of her house as I pull the door open. Evan would have a fit if I ever left our house open like this. I can't imagine Miles letting her get away with it. Although, she's worse than me. I'm sure she doesn't listen to what he has to say often.

"I brought mint chip ice cream and Skinny Pop!" I say excitedly, although, I hate the taste of this popcorn. But Sierra thinks that she won't gain weight from eating it, even though she practically lives on it.

"Yay!" She stands from the couch and grabs the sack out of my hands and then heads toward the kitchen.

I follow behind her. "How's everything going? You been feeling alright?" I have to admit that I love being pregnant with her. She's only about a month further along than I am.

"Eh, I'm alright. I'm ready for this kid to come out though." She chuckles as she grabs two waters from the fridge.

"Uh, Sierra? You still have awhile." I laugh. "Is it really that bad?"

She rubs her belly.

"Miles is just gone all the freaking time, and I'm so tired, and I just need a break."

"Sier, why didn't you tell me? I'm happy to help any time I can, and Evan loves kids."

She sniggers. "Well, that's good considering he's going to have one soon." I had no idea she had been so stressed. Now I feel like a super shitty friend. "But no, I'm fine. I just miss my husband. I thought that since he's home now, I'd see him more, but I feel like he's never here.

Miles was sent overseas soon after they got married. He didn't meet their son until he was close to a year old. I know that they desperately love each other, but I imagine the stress of being away from each other for so long, really did a number on their relationship. I can't fathom the idea of being away from Evan for such a long period of time.

"Well, just know that I'm here to help any way I can, okay?"

"Thanks, babe." She grabs the popcorn out of the microwave and pours us each a bowl. "Anyway, let's go watch a sappy ass movie and pretend we're drinking wine. Shall we?"

I laugh. "Sounds good."

"How's work going?" Sierra asks as she flips through Netflix, looking for a movie to watch.

"Ugh." I moan. "I'm so over Charlotte and her bullshit." I roll my eyes even though she's not looking at me.

"What did the bitch do now?" She's never met anyone I work with, but she's heard me complain enough to know I can't stand my boss.

"We have this huge project coming up, which is making her even bitchier than normal."

"Is that going to keep you there later every night?"

I sigh. "Yeah, most likely."

"Girl, your husband adores you, but I'll be the first to tell you he's going to shit a brick knowing you're working late at that place. He hates that you work there."

If that isn't the truth. It's not that my husband doesn't support what I do, but he hates how hard they work us, and he's not crazy about where it's located. Don't get me wrong. There're definitely worse areas in Phoenix, but I've seen my share of crazy people over the years I've been there.

"I love him, but it drives me crazy when he acts like that." I'm being a total bitch, but I guess this is my way of justifying the fact that I work for Kinsley. Although, I can't imagine not working there though because I love all the friends I've made. Especially Carly. "Plus, what would I do all day if I wasn't working? It's not like the baby is here yet to keep me busy."

We finally decide to watch *A Walk to Remember*, which is a shitty choice considering we're both hormonal pregnant women. She gets up at least four times to pee, and I'm pretty sure I've gone just as many times. I can only imagine how it's going to be once I'm further along.

"Honey, I'm home!" Miles hollers from the front door. I don't think Sierra realized how early he'd be home or she would have kicked me out by now.

"Babe, what are you doing home?" She gives him a confused look.

"They let us go early tonight since we have an early day tomorrow. What are you girls up to?" He leans in to kiss his wife on the lips and then bends down to give me a hug.

"Just watching chick flicks and talking about our controlling husbands," I answer with a wink.

He clutches his chest in mock offense. "What? We are so not controlling. But where's my dinner, woman?" He chuckles.

Sierra grabs a handful of popcorn and throws it at his head, which has me and Miles both laughing. It's clear they love each other, even if they struggle sometimes. What couple doesn't? Although, mine and Evan's marriage is probably as close to perfect as you can get. I don't take that for granted. We both wanted children much sooner than now, but had we been successful before, I'm not sure our relationship would be as strong as it is.

I laugh and stand from the couch. "Alright, you two lovebirds. I'm going to head home so you can have sexy time." I waggle my eyebrows.

"Girl, he will *not* be getting sexy time from me until he washes his smelly ass." These two always have me cracking up. They remind me a lot of me and Evan.

"Yeah, go back to watching your movie. I'll have my way with my *sweet* wife when you girls are done." He winks at Sierra, and she sticks her tongue out at him as he heads down the hallway toward their bedroom.

She sighs as she leans back into the couch and props her feet up on the table.

"You guys are freaking adorable," I say as she hits play on the movie.

She laughs. "He's a pain in the ass, but he's my pain in the ass."

❦ 4 ❧

EVAN

"Goddamn it!" I holler at myself in frustration as I slam my pen down on the big oak desk. I've been working in Scottsdale since early this morning. I had been hoping to leave here around dinner time so I could spend the evening with my wife, but this case is far from being finished.

I've worked for Howser & Bowman law firm, as a family attorney, since the year before me and Avery got married. I really lucked out with how fast I found work after finishing school. I know that typically it takes much longer. Especially in a place like Phoenix.

I dig my phone out of my suit pocket to see if Avery has texted me yet today. I know that Kinsley is starting a big project, so she's going to be even busier than normal. I'm proud of her for going after her dream of being an interior designer, but I fucking hate the people she works for. I know she doesn't put up with their bullshit, but really to an extent, she does because she thinks she has to work. Once she's further along in her pregnancy, I'm really hoping she'll agree to quit so she can stay home with the baby. Both of my parents were always working when me and Claire were growing up, and we hated it. A crew of different nannies basically raised us until we were old enough to stay home by ourselves. I refuse to allow someone else to raise my child.

It's six o'clock, and who knows when I'll actually get to leave this damn place. Flynn Howser, my boss, asked me to come to Scottsdale today because they wanted someone with experience helping them with this child custody case. I absolutely hate when there are children in the middle of their parents' bullshit. Thankfully, with the Donald case, there isn't any physical abuse, but it is for sure a nasty divorce, and they've pulled their three innocent children right into the center of it. I'm not looking forward to their court date.

My phone vibrates on the desk next to me.

"Hey Av," I say in way of greeting. After spending the entire day locked up with her yesterday, I miss her like crazy. "Did you make it home alright?" I know I'm overprotective of her, but I don't care. I'll never stop worrying about her or our child she's carrying. I know I'm going to piss her off way more times than I can count, but she'll just have to get used to it.

"I'm at Sierra's for a girls' night. We're eating popcorn and ice cream."

I chuckle. "You two are trouble." Sierra was my sister's roommate when she was in the hospital a couple years ago. They quickly became friends, and in turn, Avery gained another, too. She didn't really have a lot of friends outside of work, so I was glad for it.

"Have you left Scottsdale yet?" I hear her crunching on

the other line. Her cravings are insane. I can't even tell you how many times I've had to leave the house late at night to get her something strange. I'm talking like orange juice and cheese crackers. Nobody warned me of that nonsense.

I sigh. "No." I run my hands through my hair that desperately needs to be cut. "I'm going to be here for another hour or so. You think you can stay with Sierra until I get back to town?"

"We just started our movie, so I'm sure that won't be a problem. But you know I'm a big girl, right, Mr. Porter?" She chuckles at me. She knows I'm overprotective and often gives me shit about it, but after much arguing, I usually get my way.

"Yes, Mrs. Porter, I know you're a big girl. But that doesn't mean I'll ever stop taking care of you. I love you, baby momma." She hates when I call her that, but I find it entertaining getting a rise out of her.

"Evan Porter, if you ever want to have more children, you better watch your mouth." I hear the humor in her tone.

"So feisty," I mumble. "I gotta get back to work, but be careful if you decide to leave. Please?" Sierra's house isn't in the nicest part of town, and I'd really prefer if she didn't drive home before I get back into Phoenix. But my wife is very independent, and so I try to find some middle ground.

"Promise. Love you." I hear her make kissing noises into the phone, and I laugh.

"I love you, too. I'll see you tonight."

"Mr. Porter?" I look up from my desk and see a blonde woman who appears to be in her mid-twenties. She's wearing a form-fitting skirt and a white buttoned-up shirt that causes her cleavage to practically spill out of the top. She doesn't look like she's dressed for work, but what do I know?

"You must be Mallory." I stand from my chair and lean over the desk to shake her hand.

"Yeah, my uncle said that I'd find you back here."

"I'm sorry. Your uncle?" Nobody told me that she was related to anyone in the office. Great, just what we need. I hope to God that she knows what she's doing and they didn't just hire her because she's family.

"Yes, Flynn is my uncle. On my mother's side." *Wonderful.*

"Nice to meet you." She seems nice enough. I just hope she can handle the workload I'll be giving her. "You're okay with working in Phoenix most days? I'm only in Scottsdale once or twice a week whenever they need an extra hand here."

"It's no problem. I live in Phoenix."

"Great. Did Flynn already give you a laptop?"

"He did. Do you want me to set it up in here?"

"That won't be necessary. Tonight, I just need a little bit of filing done, and then you can head out. I won't keep you late."

I grab the box on the floor next to my desk and start pulling the files out. This place is so ancient, it isn't even funny. Thank God our office in Phoenix is higher tech than this one.

"They are all in alphabetical order and so are the three cabinets. It shouldn't take you long."

After I set Mallory up, I head out to the break room to fill up on coffee.

I fill my travel mug, and as I'm putting cream in it, Malcom walks in with a grin on his face.

"What the hell is wrong with you?" I ask as I stir my cup.

"Man, your assistant is *hot*." He wiggles his eyebrows, and I shake my head at him.

"Are you ever going to grow up?" I laugh. "You could be married with kids by now, but no woman wants to deal with your crazy ass." And it's true. Malcom Jefferies is a complete man-whore. Women like him until he opens his mouth.

"Whatever." He smirks as he pours his own cup. "Give me two weeks, and I guarantee I'll have her in bed."

I don't know why I'm friends with this guy. Although, Avery can't stand him, so we never see much of each other outside of work. Not that I blame her. The guy is a real moron.

I head back to my office, and I see Mallory quickly sticking her phone down her shirt.

"Are you about done with the files?" I ask as I check my own phone to see if Avery has called or texted again. I'm desperate to get out of here soon so I can get home to my wife. I hate these long days when we don't get to see each other. I left home this morning before she was awake.

"Yep."

She puts one last document into the cabinet and then sets the empty folder on my desk.

"Great. You're free to go now. I'll be back in the Phoenix office tomorrow around eight o'clock, but you don't need to be there until eight-thirty."

"Sounds good, Mr. Porter."

Forty-five minutes later, I'm finally on my way home to Avery, and I want nothing more than to spend the rest of the night under the sheets with her. I know I'm acting like a teenage boy who has never gotten laid before, but I don't think I'll ever get enough of my wife.

❈ 5 ❈

AVERY

TWO MONTHS LATER

"Want to see a movie or something after dinner?" Evan asks as we pull into our favorite Mexican place. It's been an extremely busy week for both of us at work, and we're finally able to spend some time together.

"Honestly, I kind of just want to go home and put my pajamas on and watch a movie. I'm really tired." I turn in my seat to look at him. *Damn, he's sexy.*

I'm six months pregnant now and still just as tired as I was when I first found out.

"Whatever you want." He finds a parking spot, and after he shuts the car off, leans over the armrest, rubs his calloused hand along my face, and then pulls me into a searing kiss. I'll never tire of this man and his romantic ways.

He releases me from our kiss and looks into my eyes. "I love you." He gives me his sexy grin.

"And I love you." I quickly peck his cheek and then open my door to get out.

"Hold on, Av. Claire is calling me." I pull the door shut. I'm glad that him and Claire have a better relationship now. It was a bit rocky when she first moved here a couple years ago, but they've since gotten closer. They try to meet up for lunch once a week. I wish I had that kind of relationship with my sister, Ainsley. I guess if she didn't live in San Diego, we probably would.

"Hey, sis," he says as an answer. "What? Claire, calm down. I can't understand you." I turn in my seat as I try to make out the words that she's saying on the other end of the line but all I hear is crying. *What is going on?*

"Ev, what's wrong?" He doesn't answer me but puts a finger in his ear, obviously trying to hear what she's saying.

"Fuck. We're on our way." He quickly pulls out of our parking spot, tires squealing. It's truly a miracle that there aren't any cops around, because we'd be in deep shit right now.

He ends the call and grips the steering wheel tight, his knuckles turning white. I'm slightly afraid that he's going to snap it in two because of how hard he's clutching it.

"Ev, what the hell is going on? Are they okay?" I'm scared to know the answer but ask anyway.

"No." He shakes his head, seeming to be in shock from whatever Claire just told him.

I desperately want to pry, but think better of it. I decide to let him gather himself before making him tell me what's going on. Obviously, something bad has happened. I just pray that the kids are alright.

I'm a bit nervous at the fact that he's driving while he's this upset.

"Babe, pull over, and I'll drive."

The next thing I know, he's pulling into the parking lot of a vacant building. He quickly pulls the gear into park.

I grab the handle to get out to switch seats with him, but he stops me by finally speaking.

"There was a fire." Is all he says, and those four words have my mind going a million miles an hour.

"Are Claire and the kids alright?" I feel like I'm going to throw up while I wait for his answer. It seems like an hour before he responds, although it's probably only a few seconds.

"Yeah, they are fine." He sighs. "It's Sierra and Miles."

Oh, God. I can't breathe.

"Are- are they okay?" I cry, and my vision is immediately blurry from my tears.

Evan turns in his seat and grabs my head.

"Miles didn't make it," he whispers. My heart immediately cracks in my chest for one of my best friends.

"No." I gasp. "Is- is Sierra alright? Auggie?" I search his eyes for any sort of answer.

"Auggie was with Claire, but Sierra is in the hospital. They're worried she's going to go into preterm labor." He squeezes my hand.

"We need to go to the hospital. Now!" I cry in hysterics.

"Av, you need to calm down. You're getting worked up, and it's not good for the baby." He looks at me with worry etched on his face. "We'll go see her, but it's not going to do her any good if you're upset like this." A part of me wants to scream at him that of course I'm upset because one of my closest friends just lost her husband and now her and her baby are at risk. I decide against it because I have no energy to argue with him.

Instead of responding, I turn in my seat, and I start to practice my breathing techniques that my therapist taught me in high school. I try to think of things that make me happy and calm while my eyes are closed. I then slowly open my eyes and turn to look at him.

"Better?" he asks gently.

I answer with a nod. He seems to be calmer now that he's told me what happened.

I'm not sure what details Evan has, but frankly, I don't want to know them anyway. Not now, at least.

We're about halfway through our drive when I start mindlessly rubbing at my protruding stomach.

"Love you, baby girl," I whisper and then see Evan slightly turn toward me, out of the corner of my eye. I'm momentarily embarrassed that he just heard me speaking to our unborn child, but then that thought slips away as soon as he places his big hand on my stomach.

"Daddy loves you too, princess, and can't wait to meet you soon," he says as he reaches over and rubs my belly. I turn and look at him and see a small smile grace his handsome face.

I give him a forced smile in return, but I know it doesn't reach my eyes. I'm sure he can tell that it isn't genuine but that I'm trying.

"Hey," he grabs my hand off my bump. "I don't know what's going to happen today, but we're going to get through this together, alright?" I don't know how he does it, but this man always has a way of calming me through any storm or battle I face.

"Okay," I whisper and then draw small circles on his hand as I rest my head on the window for the rest of the drive.

———

THE REMAINDER of our drive is quiet. As soon as we make it to the hospital, Evan pulls in front of the building and hands the valet workers the keys to the Jeep and then escorts me inside.

"You okay?" he asks into my hair as he drapes his arm around my waist. He kisses the side of my head, and I try relaxing into him.

"I will be. I just need to see that she's alright," I say almost inaudibly.

We stop at the front desk to ask what floor Sierra is on and then head toward the elevators located near the entryway. This hospital is huge, so it takes a few minutes to make it up to the eighth floor. Of course, we have to stop several times to pick up others on our way up. We stand side by side huddled together while he whispers reassuring words into my ear.

Finally, the elevator comes to a stop and dings before the door opens to the floor we need. Evan grabs my hand possessively and pulls me toward the waiting room that sits down the hall.

"Claire!" I cry as my sister-in-law grabs me into a tight, almost suffocating hug. "Have you heard anything?" I pull away from her as I dab at the tears that have started to fall again. I'm sure I look a mess right now, but I just need to know that my friend is alright.

"They haven't let us see her yet." She sniffs as she pulls

away and then sits back down next to Ryke. He wraps his arms around her shoulder, and I'm glad she has him here with her.

"Where's Auggie?"

"Ryke's parents were in town for dinner, so they have all the kids at our house."

Evan grabs me into a hug and then tells us that he's going to get us all coffee. I think he just needs a moment to himself. He and Miles weren't great friends, but we've all hung out a lot over the months since he got home. Sierra was always worried that something would happen to him while he was overseas. I'm sure she never imagined something like this happening.

My husband comes back minutes later with four coffees. He hands them out and then grabs my hand as he takes the empty chair next to me.

I sip on the warm, sugared drink, but it's hard to taste it right now. Until I know what's going on with Sierra and her baby, I'm not going to have much of an appetite.

❧ 6 ❧

AVERY

It's been two weeks since the fire, and Sierra had a precious, thankfully healthy, little boy the same day. Today, she finally gets to leave the hospital. She, of course, lost her house, along with her husband, so she is going to stay with us for a bit. We weren't sure if she'd decide to stay in Phoenix, and we didn't want to ask her, so we thought this was the best option for them right now. I've already told work that I would be out for at least a week more. There's no way she'll be able to take care of both boys yet. Thankfully, Claire will be able to help as well.

She has refused to leave the hospital without the baby, so Claire and I have been taking care of Auggie. The little guy is only two, but it's obvious that he knows something is wrong. He has for sure missed his momma. Against Sierra's wishes, we also set her up with a therapist that has been visiting her three times a week. She has yet to talk to any of us, so I'm guessing she hasn't spoke to the therapist either, but hopefully, she'll start to open up soon. I can't even begin to imagine what she's going through.

"Hey, Momma. You ready to go?" I ask as Claire and I walk into her room. She's already in a wheelchair, holding her sleeping baby.

She doesn't say anything but turns toward us and gives us a weak smile. It breaks my heart seeing my friend like this, and I know Claire feels the same way.

Claire wheels her out as I carry the few things she had with her.

The walk to my car is silent. I lift the baby and his carrier into the backseat and place it in the base that is already strapped into the seat.

Claire helps her out of the wheelchair and into the backseat. I'm hoping that she'll get some good rest now that she'll be at my house. I don't imagine she slept great in that godawful bed in the hospital the last couple weeks.

As soon as we get to the house, Evan meets us in the garage and lifts the baby out of the car to carry him inside. Claire leaves to get Auggie, and Sierra mindlessly goes to the spare room we have set up for her. I decide that I'll just let her be for now. I know the little one will want to eat soon, so I'll have to find his bottles and have one ready for him.

"How's she doing?" Evan asks as he sets the baby's car seat on the floor and then starts to unbuckle him. "Should I take him out?"

"Yeah, I'm sure he'll be hungry soon. He'd probably like to be rocked, too." I give him a small smile. It melts my heart every time I see him with a baby. I can't imagine how I'll feel when I see him with our daughter.

He lifts the little guy up into his arms and then carefully walks him to the rocking chair in the corner of the room, and I sit across from them on the couch.

"Sierra still isn't talking much. I'm really worried about her. I know that if she was in a better state of mind, she'd be mad at herself for not taking care of her boys. I honestly don't know what to do to help her." I shake my head and feel the tears prick at my eyelids. I hate seeing my friend like this.

"Simon's dad is a psychologist. Maybe he could help us." I know I don't always give him credit for it, but he's fucking amazing.

"You're the best, babe. I love you. You know that, Evan Porter?" I look at him and now have tears running down my face. I think I desperately need to get some rest because all of the stress from the last couple weeks is finally starting to catch up to me. But I need to be here to help with the boys.

"Why don't you go take a bath and lay down for a bit?" I can tell he's worried about me, but I really need to be up in case they need me.

"I'll be okay." I slowly stand from the couch and walk over to kiss him on the top of his head then lean over and kiss the baby on his cheek.

"Okay, well, if you start feeling bad, I want you in bed, alright?" He looks at me, obviously expecting me to argue with him.

"Promise." I wink at him and then start toward the kitchen to get a bottle ready.

"What's this little guy's name?" I turn around, and Evan is holding the baby's little finger, and my heart nearly explodes in my chest.

"I don't know what she decided on. I'm not sure he has a name yet."

It makes me so sad to think about how the first couple

weeks of this little boy's life, his mom hasn't been able to enjoy him because she's been so lost in her grief. Her and Miles were so excited about having another boy. Damn it. I wish he were here so things could be perfect again for her. She was so in love with that man. I can't imagine how I would handle something so horrific happening to Evan.

I push the thought out of my mind, as I don't need to make myself even more emotional than I already am.

I find the can of formula and quickly read the instructions to make sure I'm adding the correct amount with the water.

I carefully empty the powder into the bottle, and then just as I go to shake it, I hear little wails coming from the other room.

"Shh, shh, little one. It's coming." My husband coos into his ear.

Evan has the baby propped up on his shoulder while he pats at his little butt, trying to comfort him.

"Hey," I whisper, "want me to take him?" I rub his little back and then inhale his sweet little newborn scent. It's evident that the hospital staff bathed him in lavender before he left.

"I'll feed him," he says without looking up. "I need all the practice I can get." He finally looks up and gives me a small smile. "Why don't you go lay down? Claire won't be back with Auggie for a bit. She said she'd feed him dinner first."

I tell Evan to make sure he burps the baby and then decide that I should stop being stubborn and listen to him.

I leave the room and head toward our bedroom and immediately collapse onto our bed. I'm trying to be strong for my best friend, but the stress of the last couple of weeks has finally caught up to me.

I slowly pull myself off the bed, feeling like I could really use a bath right about now.

After stripping out of my clothes, I spend the next half hour in the tub, being soothed by the sight of my baby girl bouncing around inside of me.

IT'S NOW BEEN three days since we brought Sierra and her boys to stay with us. After the first night, I finally found out the baby's name. She named him Jayce Miles. Miles's middle name was Jayce, so I thought it was perfect.

"Hey sweetie, want to go with me to the store? I thought we could do some baking tonight." I really want to get her out of the house, but I've also desperately been wanting oatmeal raisin cookies.

"Yeah, I'd like that." She sits up in her bed and gives me a half smile. "I'm sorry I've been such a horrible friend, I just feel so numb," she whispers and then wipes at the lone tear that slips from her eye.

I tell her to scoot over, and then I join her and grab her hand. "Sier, you have been the furthest thing from a horrible friend. You just experienced something that no woman should ever have to go through, and on top of that, your body has gone through a lot with having the baby." I wrap her in a tight hug. "I know it's hard to believe right now, but you're going to get through this. We're all here for you. You know that, right?" I turn to look at her and then kiss the top of her head.

"Yeah," she sighs. "I don't know how I would have

made it this far without all of you. Seriously, Av. I had nowhere to go. You guys could have left me out on the street, but you didn't." She rests her head on the headboard.

"It was tempting, but we'd never do that." I wink at her, and I'm thankful for the small giggle that comes from her. I don't think I've heard her laugh since before the accident.

"Love you, girl," she leans her head on my shoulder, "thanks for everything."

"I love you, too, my sister from another mister."

7

AVERY

I shoot up in bed, feeling like someone is stabbing me in the side. I'm sweating, and my head is spinning, and I don't realize that Evan is trying to get my attention.

"Av, what's wrong?" I slowly look toward my husband, surely with panic etched on my face.

I'm breathing heavily, causing me to not be able to answer him right away.

"I- I think I'm in labor." This cannot be happening. I'm only thirty-three weeks pregnant.

Before I can say anything else, Evan is out of bed, throwing his pants and shirt on from yesterday. The next thing I know, I'm being lifted from the bed, and then he is slipping a shirt over my head.

"We're going to the hospital." He brings me my pair of slip-on tennis shoes, and I quickly grab my phone off the bedside table, knowing I'll need to call Dr. Cooper on the way.

As I'm about to exit our bedroom, the sharp pain hits me again, and I bend over from the intensity of it. *What the hell is going on?* I've heard all about Braxton Hicks contractions, but this is way more painful than anyone ever told me about. There's no way I can be having this baby already.

"Come on, Av." The pain hasn't subsided yet, but Evan lifts me in his arms and, in the next minute, into the car.

He quickly calls the hospital to let them know we're on our way and demands they have a room waiting for me as soon as we get there. If I weren't feeling so incredibly shitty, I'd tell him to calm the hell down, but right now, I'm feeling the exact same way.

As soon as we arrive at the hospital, I'm being escorted to a room in a wheelchair. Once I'm on the extremely uncomfortable bed, the staff hooks me up to a heart monitor, and then my arm is being wrapped in a blood pressure cuff. My mind is spinning, the unknown terrifying me. I just need to know that my baby girl is alright.

I start to panic as I realize that Evan is no longer in the room.

"Where's my husband?" I yell out. If they made him leave, does that mean something is wrong?

"It's okay, Mrs. Porter. We just had him go to the front desk to fill out your paperwork. He'll be back shortly."

It makes me angry that they felt the damn paperwork was more important than me having my husband by my side, but I'm in too much pain to say anything else.

After telling me that the baby's heart rate is fine but my blood pressure is slightly elevated, I'm left alone and told a doctor will be in soon to see me. I'm still having some contractions but not nearly as bad as when we were at home.

"Hey, Av," Evan says as he walks in, looking haggard

after working so many late nights recently. I just realized that it's three in the morning. I would tell him to go home to sleep for a few hours before he has to go to work, but I know it would fall on deaf ears. There's no way he'd leave me here.

"Hey." I give him a weak smile. "I'm sorry for scaring you." I lay my head back on the pillow and sigh.

He comes to the side of the bed and grabs my hand. "You didn't do anything wrong. Sure, you and this little girl," he rubs my large bump, "just took five years off of my life, but I'm glad that it looks like she'll be staying in there a bit longer."

We're interrupted when there's a knock on the door.

"Mrs. Porter, I'm Dr. Johansen. I'm the on-call doctor tonight." He shakes mine and Evan's hands, and I give him a weak smile. I need him to stop with the formalities and reassure me that my baby is alright.

"Doctor, is everything alright with my wife and baby?" The concern on my husband's face breaks my heart, but I can't worry about that. All I can worry about right now is my child.

"Yes. It appears that the little princess wanted to give you both a scare tonight, but we'll make sure she finishes cooking first." He chuckles, and I'm internally rolling my eyes, and I'm pretty sure that Evan wants to reach out and strangle the guy right now. When he sees that we're not amused, he goes on, "Avery, I would like you to go on bedrest for the remainder of your pregnancy."

I gasp. "But you just said everything is fine?" I'm freaking out because I'm supposed to be cooking Thanksgiving dinner for everyone at our house in a couple weeks, but that won't be possible now.

"Everything is fine, but if you don't take it easy, I'm worried that she's going to try to come early again. We would like to see you go for another four weeks."

He gives us a few more instructions, and then we're told that a nurse will be in to give me something to stop the contractions. I won't be able to do anything until this child is born. I know that this is what's best for our baby, but I'm freaking the hell out thinking about everything I was hoping to get done before she arrived.

It's the week after Thanksgiving, and I'm starting to really lose my mind from boredom. At first, it was easy for me to relax, even though I felt useless not being able to do anything, but now, I'm starting to go stir crazy. Evan bought me a new Kindle and an Amazon gift card to purchase new books on it, but after a while, I got sick of laying around.

My phone rings from the coffee table in front of me. I carefully lean over to grab it. Nowadays, it's becoming harder and harder each day to move. I'm thirty-six weeks pregnant today, and so that means I only have one more week before the doctor is okay with me delivering.

"Hello?" I ask, struggling to catch my breath. Damn, this kid is literally knocking the wind out of me.

"Hey, girl. How are you feeling?" Claire asks from the other end. She's been calling almost every day since I was put on bedrest, even though Sierra and her boys are now staying with her. She's somehow found a way to make sure I don't go completely insane being locked up in the house.

"Oh, you know. Like I've got a tiny human inside of me, trying to kick her way through me." I've always been a smart ass, but I must say, being as pregnant as a whale has made me even more of one.

She chuckles. "I'm so glad you're doing good."

I roll my eyes even though she can't see me.

"What are you doing? How are my niece and nephew?"

"They're good." She gives me a short answer, which has me wondering what's going on.

"What's wrong?"

She sighs. "Sierra just told me that her and the boys are moving to Carolina Beach to live with her grandma." I hear her sniffling. "I know we kind of expected this, but I don't want her to go."

"Oh, my God." Sierra quickly became one of my best friends, along with Claire, so the thought of her leaving breaks my heart. "When are they leaving?"

"This weekend. She's already got their plane tickets, so she's pretty much ready to go."

"She's flying across the country with a toddler and newborn by herself?" The thought makes me cringe. I'm scared to death to only have one. I can't imagine trying to handle more than that, by myself, nonetheless.

"Yeah. Me and Ryke offered to drive them out there, but she said she'd be fine traveling on her own with the boys."

I rest my head on the back of the couch.

"God. I'm gonna miss her." I sigh. "I know it has to be painful for her to be here without Miles."

"At least she won't have to work for a while. Miles made sure she was taken care of in case anything happened to him overseas. Nobody ever considered something like this happening to him instead."

"Yeah, that's good."

Sierra doesn't have a lot of family around anymore. Her dad abandoned her mom, her, and her two younger brothers when she was eight. A few years after that, her mom went off the deep end and left Sierra, Clay, and Owen with their grandmother. She raised the three of them, but after Sierra graduated from high school and her grandfather died, her grandmother decided to move to Carolina Beach. She, of course, stayed behind because of Miles, but now I can't imagine how hard it is to be here.

"I know you're on bedrest, but I want to do something, just the three of us, before she leaves."

"Yeah, definitely. I know Evan won't let me leave the house, but you girls can come over here if you want. We could order Chinese and watch stupid comedies or something."

She laughs. "That sounds perfect." She pauses. "I just can't imagine not having her around anymore, you know? I wish things were different."

"Me too. Who knows? Maybe she'll come back after taking a break from Phoenix for a bit." I think being around her grandma could be good for her. Plus, I'm sure she'll like being close to her brothers again, and it'll be good for her boys to have their uncles to do some of the things that Miles would have done with them.

After talking for a few minutes, we hang up so Claire can take care of Brady and Aria. The thought of not having Sierra and her boys around anymore makes me sad. I was really hoping that the three of us could all raise our kids together. But now that won't be possible, with her being clear across the country.

"Hey," Evan says as he walks into the living room, donned in a slate grey suit and black dress shoes. The man is sexy as sin.

"Hey." I try to stand from the couch, but then flop back in defeat when I realize that it's too much work.

"Rough day?" he asks as he takes the seat next to me and pulls me into his arms. "Is our princess treating her mommy good today?" He rubs at my stomach, which seems to be one of his favorite things to do these days.

"No. I'm pretty convinced that she already hates me, and she's not even born yet."

He chuckles. "Nah. I've heard that doesn't happen until at least the teen years."

"Well then, she needs to start being nicer to me." I laugh. "I just got off the phone with Claire."

"Oh, yeah? What'd she want?" He strokes my ponytail that desperately needs to be washed. Damn. A shower sounds wonderful about now, but the thought of having to stand for any amount of time, makes me quickly change my mind.

"Sierra and the boys are moving to her grandma's in North Carolina."

He raises his eyebrows. "Really? I mean, I guess we shouldn't be surprised, but damn."

"I know. I think it'll be good for her to start over after everything, but I'm going to miss her like crazy."

"Well, maybe we can all make a trip out there this summer." This is another reason I love this man.

"Really? That would be awesome." I smile up at him.

"Hey, you think you could help me get in the shower? I smell like hell, but I don't think I can do it by myself."

He gives me a Cheshire grin, and I roll my eyes at him.

"Have I ever denied you when you offered to be naked in front of me?"

"Evan! I'm thirty-six weeks pregnant and bigger than a house. Tell junior to calm the hell down." I smirk at him, knowing he's going to lecture me for the nickname I just gave his dick.

He leans into my ear. "Avery Porter, there's nothing junior about my dick, and I don't give a fuck how big you think you are. I'll always find you sexy as hell." He bites down on my earlobe, which has me yelping, and then he pecks me on the cheek before standing from the couch to help me up.

He holds his hand out to me. "Come on. Let's go shower." He looks at me, obviously expecting me to argue with him. "Don't argue, because you won't win, Av. I want to see you naked." He wiggles his eyebrows at me.

"You're insatiable." I mumble under my breath as he pulls me to stand.

"Don't you forget it."

He swats at my ass as we walk to the bathroom.

"Mr. Porter, it's going to be at least a couple months before I can have sex again, but if you'd like to make it longer, keep that shit up."

"Fine. I'll be good." He huffs and rolls his eyes at me.

I smirk at him, and then we make our way to the shower.

THE NEXT NIGHT, Claire and Sierra come over so we can hang out one last time.

"Damn, I'm going to miss you." I lean my head against Sierra's shoulder.

"I'll miss you guys too. I really hate leaving, but I just feel like I need to start somewhere fresh without all the memories. You know?"

I turn to look at her, now feeling like a bitch for making her feel bad.

"I completely understand, Sier. I can't imagine how you feel right now. You need to be with your family. But you better believe that we're going to bug the hell out of you by visiting way too much."

"Hell yes!" Claire chimes in, which has me and Sierra laughing. She never used to talk like this until she moved to Phoenix. I know, I'm a terrible influence.

"I hope you guys do. My grandma is right on a private beach, which is so amazing because hardly anyone else hangs out on it. Only about ten houses have access to it."

"That does sound amazing."

"I'm sorry I won't be here when the baby is born." I look over at her, and her eyes glisten with unshed tears.

"Girl, don't you dare apologize. As soon as she's here, we'll FaceTime so you can see her."

"Okay." She nods. "I just feel bad because you all have been here so much for me, and now, I feel like I'm bailing on you guys."

Claire chimes in, "Sierra Greene, stop that right now. You are not bailing on us."

We order take-out and find an old movie on Netflix that stars Nicolas Cage and Cher. It's ridiculously cheesy, but has Sierra laughing, so I'm happy.

"Promise me that you'll text one of us as soon as you land, so we know you made it okay," I say as I hug Sierra one last time before her and Claire leave to go back to her house.

"I promise." She squeezes me tight. The sadness still radiates off of her, but I'm glad that she was at least able to have a little bit of fun tonight. We were all in desperate need of a girls' night.

"We'll start looking for hotels along the beach to come visit this summer," Claire says, and I nod my head in agreement.

"I can't wait. And I'm guessing by then I'll want to stay in a hotel with all of you because Grandma Rose is probably going to be getting on my last nerves." She laughs, which has me and Claire laughing right along with her.

"Love you, girl," I say as they walk out of the front door. "Everything is going to be great in NC, I promise."

She gives me a big, forced smile, but I'll take it. There was a time where she wasn't even able to pretend she was happy.

8

EVAN

"Love you. Have a good day." I kiss Avery's forehead before making my way out of our bedroom. I still don't feel comfortable leaving her on her own, but thankfully, my sister checks in on her when she can.

"You too." I hear her grumble, and I chuckle. My girl is definitely not a morning person.

I fill my to-go mug with coffee and then head to work. I got a call last night from Flynn telling me that we were having an office meeting first thing this morning. I don't know why he felt the need to tell me, instead of letting me find out with everyone else today. His odd behavior hasn't gone unnoticed over the last couple weeks. Typically, he takes on any and all clients, but recently, he's been turning more and more down. I know we've been busy, but it's unusual for him to deny anyone.

I pull into my reserved spot and then shoot Avery a quick text, telling her I love her again. What can I say? That woman has turned me into a pussy.

Avery: Love you;) Chinese tonight?

I chuckle to myself, because all she's wanted to eat lately is greasy egg rolls, but I can't deny her anything, even if I wanted to.

Me: Sounds good. Take care of my princess and call if you need anything.

I leave my phone on, not wanting to miss a call from her if she needs me.

"Good morning, Mr. Porter." Hilary greets from behind the front desk. She's in her early sixties, so I find it strange when she acts so formal around me.

"Hilary, how many times do I have to tell you to call me Evan?" I wink at her as I walk by, and she laughs.

"You know, *Evan,* I don't think your wife would appreciate you flirting with me all the time."

I turn back toward her. "She doesn't think I'm as charming as you do." I wink again for good measure and then walk toward my office, but I'm halted by Mallory.

She tries to grab my arm, but I keep walking.

"What's wrong?" I ask, my back now toward her.

"Flynn said we're having a meeting, and it sounds pretty serious." I already knew this, but I don't tell her that.

"Where's it being held?" I ask her as I continue for my office.

"It's in conference room A. Most everyone is in there already."

When I get to my desk, I drape my suit jacket on my chair.

"I just need to send a quick email, and then I'll be in. Tell Flynn I'll only be a minute."

"Okay." She turns on her heels, and I'm left by myself.

I sigh heavily before shooting an email off to one of my clients, confirming an appointment for this week.

I look up from my computer when I hear a knock on my door.

"Evan, can I have a word with you?" Flynn asks as he takes one of the chairs across from my desk.

"Yeah, of course. Sorry, I was about to come to the conference room. I just needed to email Kent Elton to confirm his appointment for Thursday afternoon."

He shakes his head. "No, it's fine. I have everyone else in there already, but I kind of wanted to talk to you by yourself first."

That causes me to panic a bit. He sounds a little worried, which in turn, has me worried.

"Okay," I say slowly. "Is everything alright?"

I move away from the computer so I can give him my full attention.

"Yeah, everything is fine, but I'm not sure how you're going to feel about what I'm about to tell you."

"Shit, Flynn. Are you firing my ass?" I jokingly ask. I know there's no actual reason for me to lose my job. He's got a dry sense of humor at times, but I still give him a hard time occasionally. He's used to it by now.

"No, nothing like that." He clears his throat. "But," he pauses, and I kind of want to reach across my desk and strangle the guy for putting me on pins and needles.

"But? You're freaking me out, Flynn." My leg bounces under the desk, something I've always done when I'm nervous.

"I've decided to retire early, so I'll be closing the firm in June."

I shake my head. "I'm sorry, what?" I must have misunderstood him because I thought I heard him say he was closing the firm in only six months from now. I had no idea that he was even considering closing it at all.

He nods. "It's time. Mary wants to move to Cape Cod. There's nothing really here tying us down besides the firm."

"I- I don't understand. Isn't there someone you could pass it down to. What about your nephew? You said before you'd probably leave it to him. Flynn, man, you can't leave me without a job only a month before I'm expecting my first child."

I don't want to act like an ass, but he's really freaking me the hell out. I know that technically I have six months to look for a new job, but I've been here for so long. I don't want to fucking work for anyone else.

"No. I can't leave it to Garret. He'd run this place into the ground in a heartbeat, and I'd rather just close it."

I'm now seeing red as I grip the edge of the desk like my life depends on it. How the hell am I going to tell Avery about this?

"This is shit." I shake my head. "I have a baby on the way."

"I know, and that's why I wanted to tell you that Gerald's Texas office already has a job lined up for you. I told them you probably wouldn't be able to be out there for a few months because of the baby, but that works out because the position you'll be filling still has someone there until March."

Gerald Bowman was the Bowman in Howser &

Bowman until he decided to move his family to Texas ten years ago and open his own firm. For whatever reason, Flynn never changed our name. It confuses the hell out of people.

"What?" I stare at him like he has suddenly sprouted two heads, not understanding, and then I shake my head. "I can't move to Texas. There is no way in hell Avery is going to agree to this. Her family is here. I couldn't pull her away from Phoenix."

"Well, I don't need your answer yet, but I'll need it by the end of the week so I can let Dallas know." He stands to his feet. "Talk to Avery. Maybe she'll be on board with it more than you think. This could be a good opportunity for you eventually to move up when Gerald retires."

Once again, I'm stunned silent. This would be the chance of a lifetime, and it's definitely something I've wanted for a long time, but in Phoenix, not Dallas. Yeah, I have my sister and her family here, but I'm used to not being around family. But Avery is going to be a whole different story.

"I'm going to just turn you down now. I'll look around myself, but I appreciate the offer. Good luck, Flynn."

I see the look of disappointment on his face.

"If that's all you needed from me, I think I'll take the rest of the day off."

He nods and leaves my office.

I look around the small space and sigh, wondering how the hell I'm going to take care of my family now, without a job. I've worked my ass off over the years to get to where I am, but now, it feels like it's all being ripped from me in an instant.

God, how am I going to tell my wife about this?

"**W**hy did they have to kill him?" I blow my nose into a paper towel as I hiccup a cry.

"Oh, my God, Avery! You are so damn hormonal it's not even funny." Claire chuckles beside me, and I want to punch her in the face. Holy shit. I *am* hormonal.

We've been watching reruns of *Grey's Anatomy* all day. I've watched this episode probably fifteen times, but I still can't get over the fact that McDreamy died. Why? Patrick Dempsey is a fucking sex god, I mean, for an old guy, but his character is one of my all-time favorites.

"Shut up! Poor Meredith." I wipe at my wet face.

"Av, I cannot wait for this baby to be born so you can do something other than cry over fictional characters." She shakes her head at me.

"Ugh!" I throw my hands up in the air. "I've gone completely insane, haven't I?"

She moves closer to me on the couch so she can rub at my enormous belly. I'm not due until the first of the year, but my doctor said it would be safe to deliver whenever the baby decides to come. Honestly, if she gets any bigger in there, she's going to run out of room to move.

"It's okay, babe. I'll let it slide because you're pregnant, but if you're still acting this way after the baby is born, I'm having your head examined."

"Bitch," I mumble as she leaves the room chuckling.

Evan has insisted that I'm not left at home by myself, so Claire has been coming to hang out when she can.

Realizing I suddenly have to pee, I carefully lift myself off the couch. Thank God it's not super low to the ground or there'd be no way in hell I'd be able to get up on my own. Once I'm standing, an intense pain shoots through me like a lightning bolt, and I fold myself in half, hardly able to breathe.

"Holy shit." I'm trying to catch my breath when Claire walks in with Aria.

"Av, what's wrong?"

I'm unable to answer her when I notice something trailing down my leg, getting onto our new rug. *Fuck.*

"I- I think my water just broke." I notice that I'm shaking, obviously in shock from the pain. But is it just the pain? Am I ready to be a mother? What if I'm bad at it? I don't have time to doubt myself anymore because once again I feel like someone is stabbing me. *Holy shit.* If this is how my delivery is going to be, I can't do this.

Claire walks over and guides me back to the couch.

"I'm calling Evan. You need to get to the hospital."

She goes in search of her phone, but I'm unable to listen to their conversation, as the pain is overtaking my entire body.

"Okay, babe. He's going to meet us at Trinity." She

starts gathering her things and Aria, acting as if my world isn't about to completely flip upside down.

"Claire, why don't you just have him come get me here. You can't deal with me and your own child." Evan is working in town today, so it would take him no time at all to get here.

"Don't be silly." She gives Aria her sippy cup and then holds her hand out to me. "Come on. I'll help you to the car and then come back in for her."

I sigh and then take her offered hand. Terrified yet ready to get this over with and have my precious girl in my arms.

TWENTY MINUTES LATER, I'm in a room, and Evan comes sprinting in.

"Av," he pants, obviously out of breath from rushing to get here.

"I'm fine and so is the baby." I rub at my belly and then pat the spot next to me on the terribly uncomfortable bed.

"I knew I shouldn't have left you." He kisses me. "I'm so sorry."

"Stop. I'm fine. She wasn't coming until her daddy got here anyway." I wink at him, trying to lighten the mood, and it seems to be working.

"Good. I'm glad to know she's not stubborn like her mother."

I throw my head back in a laugh but then grab my stomach, the discomfort becoming too much.

"You okay?" I look up at my husband's handsome face. "Should I call for a nurse?"

I shake my head, and I'm finally able to talk. "No, it's normal. They'll be in soon to see how far dilated I am."

He nods, noticeably hating the fact that there's nothing he can do to help me right now. Having him here has made me feel better though. I just hope he doesn't divorce me after seeing how I am during labor.

"Ahh," I sigh as I close my eyes, finally able to relax. We've now been at the hospital for two hours, and the anesthesiologist just gave me my epidural. I have to admit the huge ass needle terrified me, but the thought of feeling some relief, set my mind at ease.

Evan chuckles from the chair beside my bed. "I'm glad that helped you, but I hated the idea of them sticking that fucking thing in your spine." My eyes are still closed, but I'm sure he's got his arms crossed with a pissed-off look on his face.

I open one eye to look at him, apparently too exhausted to open both.

"Ev, I'm fine. Promise." I give him a sleepy smile after seeing that I was, in fact, correct. He's definitely pissed. I won't mention to him that the fun hasn't even begun yet. Although, he should have somewhat of an idea after I dragged him to Lamaze classes.

He scoots his chair closer to me. "I'm sorry for acting like an ass, I just worry about you, gorgeous." I wish so bad that I wasn't hooked up to all these machines right now so he could join me on the bed. I'm starting to really freak out about what's to come, but having him near me, puts my mind at ease a bit.

"I love you, Evan Porter," I say as my eyes start to close again.

"I love you, too." I hear the emotion in his voice, and it breaks my heart a bit. I know he's worried about me and the baby. Maybe I should send him to get a coffee or something so he has something to do to get his mind off of it for a while. I imagine I'll be here for hours before the baby decides she wants to come. Evan said she's not stubborn like me, but I beg to differ.

Just as I'm about to drift off, the door opens and my nurse, Claudia, comes in. She's too damn chipper, and I just want to sleep.

"Hi, Avery!" Just put me out of my misery now. Is this woman going to be in here during my delivery? Because I really can't handle much more of her.

"Hi." I fake a smile.

"I'm just going to see how far dilated you are. See if little miss is getting any closer to making her grand debut."

I hear Evan shift in his seat. I know he's anxious to find out about my progress. I have a feeling I'll still be sitting at three centimeters, but I don't voice that to them. I have no freaking clue how I'm going to get my feet up in the stirrups because I can't feel the entire lower half of my body.

Nurse Claudia acts like she's new at this and just sits at my feet, waiting for me to take it upon myself. Thankfully, my amazing husband knows I can't take care of myself right now, and he helps my feet into both straps. I can feel his hands on me, but I'm pretty sure he could tickle the bottoms of my feet and I wouldn't notice. I'm half tempted to tell him to do it, because this is the one time I wouldn't deck him for tickling me.

Now that I'm spread for the world to see me, Claudia checks me out to see how far along I am. Evan squeezes my hand, and I roll my head to the side to smile at him. He leans down and kisses the corner of my mouth. I can't believe we're about to be parents in a short time. For so long, it's just been us. A part of me is sad that it won't still be like that, but the other part of me is ecstatic to start this journey with him.

I've obviously been wearing my emotions on my face. "What's going on in that head of yours?" he whispers into my ear and then taps my forehead.

"Just thinking about how crazy it is that we're going to be parents soon." I give him a sleepy smile.

I can see the moisture in his eyes, and I have a feeling that today I'm going to see a side of Evan Porter that I've never gotten to see before.

"We're going to be the best fucking parents around." We're having an intimate conversation until Claudia clears her throat. I don't care if she heard us. This is our special day, so we're allowed to say whatever the hell we want to each other.

"Alright, Avery, it looks like you're at an eight now, so it shouldn't be much longer."

There's no way I heard her right. Surely, I didn't progress that quickly. Isn't this supposed to take all day?

"Are you sure? I've only been here a couple hours." I know I sound ridiculous for asking, and when I chance a look at Evan, I can tell that he thinks I'm insane for questioning her.

Claudia laughs. "Yes, I'm sure. You have been very

fortunate with how quickly you have progressed. Usually a woman is in labor much longer than you have been, especially with her first child. But occasionally, the baby is just anxious to come." She takes off her rubber gloves and washes her hands. Before heading toward the door, she says, "I'm going to call Dr. Cooper to let him know that it's almost time. You relax for a bit because you're going to need all the energy you can muster."

FINALLY, after four long hours of pushing, we hear precious little wails fill the air. *She's here.* I throw my head back on my pillow, and that's when my own tears start to fall. After so much heartbreak from not being able to conceive for the last several years, our baby girl is finally here.

"It's a girl!" Dr. Cooper exclaims, even though we already knew.

"She's here, Av." I look up at my husband who is staring over at our daughter; a single tear slides down his cheek. My sobs come out louder now. I know I'm probably just overly hormonal right now, but this is one of the best moments of my life. *I'm a mom.*

"What does she look like?"

"Like her beautiful mother," he says as he leans down and gives me a sweet kiss. "I'm so proud of you." I reach up to his face and run my thumb along his cheek, drying his tears.

"Dad, do you want to come cut the umbilical cord?" He looks at me in question.

"Go," I smile, "then I want to hold her."

He hands his phone over to one of the nurses so he can get pictures of the first moment he shares with our daughter. She's still crying, but I've been told that it's a sign of a healthy baby, so she can cry all she wants.

After a moment, my handsome guy brings her over to me, bundled in a pink blanket.

"Here's your momma," Evan whispers as he leans her down so I can see her better. She is the most beautiful thing I have ever seen in my life, and I can't believe she's ours.

He kisses her little head and then hands her to me. I nervously take her, and I think Evan can sense my worry so he stays right next to me. I'm a bit out of it after the workout I just had.

"Hi, baby girl," I whisper into her hair, "I'm so glad you're here."

The doctor and nurses all leave, and we are able to spend our first moment together as a family of three.

🦋 10 🦋

AVERY

"Av, she's absolutely beautiful," Sierra says over the phone, and the sadness in her voice breaks my heart. Claire called her as soon as the baby was born, and it didn't take anytime for her to blow up my phone, demanding pictures.

"Thanks, Sier." There's silence on the line for a moment. "You doing okay?"

She sighs. "I'm fine, really. But this is your day, don't let me ruin it."

I throw my head back on my pillow. As excited as I am about our brand-new baby, I still worry about her. I'm closer to her and Claire than I've ever been to my own sister. I hope my daughter finds friends like them one day.

"You're not ruining my day." I decide to change the topic. "How're the boys?"

As soon as I ask, I hear a howling baby in the background and giggle.

She huffs. "Good lord, I just want to talk for five minutes."

I laugh. "Go get your baby, and I'll FaceTime you tomorrow."

"Sounds good. Love you."

I smile, even though she can't see me. "Love you, too."

As soon as I hang up, I hear footsteps clomping down the hallway, and I'm not surprised when they continue into my room.

"Let me see my niece!" Claire hollers as soon as she comes in.

"Claire, the baby is sleeping." Evan reprimands, and it has me laughing. He's already in overprotective daddy mode, and I love it.

She rolls her eyes at him. "Good luck with this one," Claire says to me as she points to her brother with her thumb.

Ryke ignores their bickering, both of us used to their arguing.

"While you two are fighting, I'm going to see how the new mom is," he says as he makes his way toward me. We all laugh. "How you feeling?" He leans down to kiss me on the cheek.

"Really good, actually. Just super tired." I could fall asleep right now, and I'm honestly exhausted from all the visitors, but I know everyone wants to see us.

He pats me on the arm and then turns toward Evan, "So, she wasn't momzilla like Claire was?" Oh shit. He's definitely sleeping on the couch tonight.

"Ryker Allen!" Claire scolds, which has us all in hysterics.

"No, she was a fucking rock star." Evan walks over to me and kisses me on the lips and then walks over and lifts the baby out of her bed.

"I forgot to even ask. What's her name?" Claire asks as she looks down at the sweet bundle in my husband's arms. We wanted her to be surprised.

Evan looks up at her so he can see her reaction. "Zoey Elizabeth."

"Really?" She gasps, and then she starts crying. Damn, we're both hormonal. "Mom would have felt so honored, and I love the name Zoey."

We finally found a name that we both loved, but then we wanted to have a part of his mom in her name so we chose Elizabeth. I can just imagine Liz looking down on her granddaughter with a huge, proud smile on her face. Her and Jack would both adore her.

After Claire and Ryke left, Evan told me about the firm closing this summer. I could tell he was hesitant about telling me, but I know he'll have no problem getting another job. He's amazing at what he does, and anyone would be lucky to have him in their practice.

"WELCOME HOME, ZO," I whisper to my sweet baby girl as we step into her nursery.

After only three days, we got the okay to go home today. She's as healthy as can be, and the doctor was happy with my recovery and didn't feel it was necessary for us to stay any longer, even with her being a few weeks early. Not all premature babies get that lucky. I'm looking forward to my own bed tonight, although, I'm not sure how much of it I'll actually be seeing anytime soon.

I carefully lower her into her crib, laying her on top of her zebra print bedding. She's been snoozing away all morning, not having a care in the world. I'm hoping this is a good sign and that she'll be easy on us.

"Why don't you let her lay in her bed and go relax on the couch while I fix you some lunch?" I look at him like he's crazy. "She'll be fine." He walks over to the dresser and grabs the baby monitor and then switches it on. "Promise. I can even watch her while I'm in the kitchen."

When we received the thing at my baby shower, I thought it was the most ridiculous invention ever, but now that she's here and I'm worried to leave her unattended, I am glad we have it.

"Okay," I sigh and follow him out of the room. Only looking back at my daughter once before exiting. I have to say I'm damn proud of myself.

Deciding that I desperately want Chinese after suffering through the tasteless hospital food the last few days, Evan orders for us.

"They'll be here in about a half hour. Want to watch a movie?"

"Sure." I nod as I yawn into my hand. I'm guessing I'll fall asleep before my beef and broccoli makes it here.

He finds an old Will Smith movie on Netflix, but before the beginning credits are over, I'm passed out.

MIDNIGHT. The sounds of little cries have me flying out of bed. I have to admit, I'm shocked that Zoey let me sleep this long. She last ate three and a half hours ago. I was told that since she's nursing, she'll eat more often than a baby who is bottle-fed.

"You got her?" Evan mumbles, clearly still half asleep.

"Yeah, babe. Go back to sleep." He'll be home from work with me for the next two weeks so I can sleep when she doesn't need to be fed. The hospital recommended that I don't start pumping until closer to time when I go back to work. That way she gets used to being on my breasts. They said that once she's tried a bottle, she most likely won't want to go back to nursing. Even as stressful as it was the first day after she was born, I'd be devastated if I couldn't do it. She's a little barracuda, and it's obvious that she's not starving.

I make my way to the nursery. At first, I was a bit hesitant to have her sleep in her crib right away, but after much reading, I learned that it could be a very difficult transition if she started out in our room. Plus, I know this sounds selfish, but we both wanted our room to remain ours.

"Hi, baby girl." I coo as I lift her from her bed. I switch on the lamp that matches her bedding before I settle us into the rocking chair in the corner of the room. "Are you hungry?"

She immediately latches on like she's starving to death, and I lean my head back, savoring this moment.

EVAN

"Evan, it was nice meeting you. I'll be in touch soon." Fred Reynolds shakes my hand and then escorts me out of his fancy ass office. I have to say the building is very upscale, but I'm not sure how comfortable I'd be working here. I like high-end, but this may be a little too much.

"Thank you, sir. I look forward to hearing from you."

I walk out into the cool December air. After spending most of my life in Chicago, it's still weird to me that it doesn't get below fifty degrees at Christmas here.

We've had Zoey home for a week now, and I have to say, it's been one of the best damn weeks of my life. Don't get me wrong. It has definitely not been easy, but Avery has been incredible. I could tell at first that she was worried that she would do something wrong as a first-time mother, but she's been nothing short of amazing.

I took two weeks off from work, and the only time I plan to leave my girls is to interview for a few jobs. The day after we got home, Fred Reynolds from Reynolds &

Sons called me after looking at my resume, and I was told he had also spoken to Flynn. I know that he feels bad about closing us down, but thankfully, he's giving us all time to find something new. Malcom and Mallory were both offered jobs in Dallas as well. I'm pretty sure Flynn felt guilty leaving his niece without a job. Although, I don't know why she would move across the country to be someone's assistant. Avery still doesn't know that I was offered a position there, but I wasn't even going to entertain the idea. I wish that she'd decide to stay home with Zoey, but she loves her job, so I know that's another thing that's tying her to Phoenix.

I head to the florist shop that Malcom's mother owns and pick up a dozen of Avery's favorite flower, purple tulips.

"Thanks, Mrs. Jefferies." I kiss her on the cheek before I turn to walk out the door.

"Give that beautiful wife of yours my love and tell her to bring that baby by once she's feeling up to it."

I nod in agreement and then make my way home to my wife and daughter.

"Av?" I ask as I walk through the front door.

"We're in here." I walk through the hallway, toward the living room, and my breath nearly hitches in my throat. The sight before me will never get old.

Avery is laying on the couch with Zoey tucked into her side as she's sound asleep, sucking on her pacifier.

"Hey," I whisper as I lean down to their level and push a stray hair away from Avery's eyes.

"Hey, you. How was your interview?" I know that she genuinely cares, but I'm relieved to know that she's not entirely stressed out about the situation like I am. I want her to enjoy being a new mother, not worry about my job, or rather lack thereof.

"I think good. I should hear back soon." I rub the back of Zoey's head and then kiss Avery on the cheek.

"That's great." She smiles up at me. "You want to hold her?"

I shake my head. "No. You two look comfortable." I stand. "I'm going to get changed out of these clothes, but I thought maybe I'd call your parents and see if they'd come hang out with her for a bit tonight." I instantly see the doubt on her face, so I hold my hand up. "We don't have to go anywhere. I just thought it would be nice to have an uninterrupted dinner together." This brings the smile back to her face. "I know you're not ready to leave her yet, and that's completely fine."

"That sounds amazing. What should we eat?"

"You think about what you'd like and I'll make it or go pick something up." I turn to walk toward our room, but then turn back to her. "But no Chinese." I wink at her and then walk away but hear her groan.

An hour later, Lucy and Ed are at the front door. My mother-in-law barges past me so she can get to the baby. She can be a bit much at times, but tonight, I know that Avery and I both appreciate them giving us a little time to ourselves. Even if Zoey will only be in the next room.

"Hey, Ed." I shake her dad's hand, and then we make our way toward the living room.

"How's my grandbaby?" he asks from behind me, and I can hear the pride in his voice.

After losing my own parents, he's the closest thing I have to a father.

"She's good and thankfully sleeps well."

When we get to the living room, Lucy is already lifting Zoey out of her bed and kissing her cheeks. She reminds me of my Great Aunt Marsha. I swear I can still feel where she used to squeeze my cheeks so hard, she'd leave marks on them for weeks.

Avery stands from the couch, where she had been reading on the Kindle I got her while she was on bed rest. I like to tease her about reading romance books, but really, it benefits me in the long run, because she's always horny as hell after reading them. Although, that does me no good right now, because according to the doctor, we can't have sex for five or six more weeks.

"You ready for our date?" I murmur into her hair, as I wrap my arms around her frame. She looks incredible, especially for only having a baby a week and a half ago. I know she doesn't feel the same way, but I've made it my mission to remind her everyday of how beautiful she is. My wife is fucking gorgeous, and she should know it.

She nods into my chest. "I'm so ready." She turns to her parents. "Thanks for coming over. We'll just be in the kitchen. She shouldn't need to eat for another couple hours."

Lucy shoos us out of the room. "We'll be right here, under the same roof. Go relax."

She doesn't have to tell us twice. I grab Avery's hand and then take her into the kitchen where I already have dinner spread out on the table.

She gasps beside me. "Babe, you did all this?"

She spins around, taking in the room. I have white lights hanging from the cabinets, with no overhead lights on. On the table, there's three red tiered candles that sit in clear glass holders, each one lit. Red rose petals are scattered around the candles.

She then starts to laugh when she notices the two pizza boxes.

"You are such a romantic."

I chuckle. "I know you've been craving sausage and mushroom pizza, so I had Tony's delivered."

She wraps her arms around my waist. "This is the best date ever."

"Ever?" I raise my eyebrows. "We're at home with your parents in the other room with our child."

She shrugs. "Still the best."

I pull her chair out for her and then kiss the top of her head before taking the seat next to her.

And it really is the best date ever. Because after we eat our pizza and make out like horny teenagers, Avery pulls me into our room and gives me the best blow job of my life.

We've now been home with Zoey for two weeks. Avery has been an absolute rock star at this whole parenting thing.

"How's Daddy's girl?" I ask my daughter as I lift her from the crib. There have been a few nights where I wished we had a bed in our room for her, but Avery convinced me that this is better in the long run. She told me enough horror stories about how hard it is to transition a baby to their crib after co-sleeping.

I have to admit that I'm surprised at how laid back this little thing is. She barely makes a peep unless she's hungry. I have a feeling that if we ever have another child, we probably wouldn't get so lucky.

I pat her back as I gently bounce her in my arms and hum a lullaby to her that I've heard Avery sing to her several times. I grab her pacifier out of the crib and one of her little blankets and make our way toward the living room. I just sent my wife away for a little bit. She's been cooped up in the house since we got home, and I could tell she was starting to get a little anxious. She reluctantly took me up on my offer after I reassured her that we would be fine. I know that she trusts me, but her motherly instinct has her thinking that she has to do everything herself. I don't want her to do everything herself.

I've been trying to convince her not to go back to work once her eight-week maternity leave is up, but I've got a fight on my hands. My woman is overly independent. I love that about her, but more than that, I'd love for her to be home with our daughter.

I prop a pillow behind my arm as I sit us on the couch. I don't know how a seven-pound baby can cause your arm to hurt so much. I rub at the dark fuzz on Zoey's head and then lean in to kiss her cheek.

"Momma needed a break so now you're stuck with your 'ol dad. You're beautiful just like her. You know that?" She grabs my finger with her little hand. I didn't know that newborns were capable of that so soon. I also never imagined myself talking to a baby like this either, but she stares up at me in awe as if she understands every word I'm saying.

I didn't know it was possible to love a little human so much, but she's already got me wrapped around her little finger.

My phone chimes from the coffee table. I pick it up and see that Avery is calling. She only just left fifteen minutes ago. I'm surprised she didn't call sooner.

"Hey, Av," I say in way of greeting.

"Hey. You two doing alright? I can come home now if you need me." I smile at her concern, but I want her to enjoy a little time away from the baby.

"No, we're just fine. We're just hanging out watching the Cardinals game. She loves them already.

She chuckles through the line. "Oh, is that right? Well, I'm glad she has good taste in football teams."

"She does. But really, go get some Christmas shopping done if you want. We'll be fine, I promise."

She sighs. "Alright. If you're sure. If she gets fussy, she's got milk ready in the fridge. You just need to heat it up in the bottle warmer."

"Av, don't worry about us. I promise I'll make sure she's taken care of."

"I know. I'm sorry."

"I want you to take care of yourself too. You're a wonderful mother and you just need a little break. There's nothing wrong with that."

"Thanks, babe. I'll be home in a couple hours."

I hit end on my phone and toss it back onto the table. Zoey is now snoozing contently in my arms, and little snores come from her nose. It's so crazy to think that we made this little thing. After so much heartache and struggle, we finally have our little angel. I hope she always knows how much me and her mother love her. I'd do anything for both my girls.

This game is boring as hell. No wonder Zoey fell asleep. I switch the TV off and then set her down in her bouncy seat. I head to the kitchen, deciding I want to make my wife something nice for dinner tonight.

I've enjoyed being home with them, but I will be going back to work tomorrow. Luckily, Christmas is next week, so I'll get another small vacation with them.

I pull the meat and different types of cheese out of the fridge that I'll need to make a lasagna. Avery does most of the cooking around here, besides when she was on bed rest, but I learned a few things from my mom growing up. This was one of my favorite dishes that she made. Damn, I miss her. I try not to think about her and my dad too much, because it makes me feel like shit, but having Zoey here, I really wish they were still around. I know I didn't always see eye to eye with them, but that didn't make their deaths any easier on me.

I quickly brown the meat on the stove and mix in all my seasonings while I boil the noodles. I think Avery will be shocked to come home to dinner waiting for her, but she deserves to be taken care of. She does so much for me and now our daughter. I want to show her how much it means to me. I can't show her in the way I'd like to right now, so dinner will have to be enough.

Once the lasagna is in the oven, I cut up vegetables for a salad and then make up a pan of brownies. Avery is careful about what she eats since she's breastfeeding, but her doctor said that it's alright to treat herself occasionally. They aren't her homemade, to-die-for brownies, but she'll still appreciate the gesture.

I go back to the other room to check on Zoey in her seat and then grab the baby monitor to make sure I hear her if she wakes.

I light a couple tall candles that Avery uses for special occasions, and then place them in the center of the table. Then I turn the dining room lights down low, to set a romantic atmosphere.

Her favorite Ed Sheeran album plays quietly in the background, and the aroma from the vanilla scented candles wafts through the air.

"What is all this?" I jump as I stand at the stove checking that the brownies are done cooking.

"Jesus, Av. You scared me." I hold my chest as I smile at her.

"Sorry." She walks toward me and then wraps her small frame around mine. "What are you making?" She eyes the food behind me.

"I thought you'd like a nice dinner after your afternoon out. Did you enjoy yourself?"

"Yeah, I did. Carly met me at the mall, and I was able to get a few things bought for Christmas." She grabs at a burnt corner of the pan of brownies, and I swat at her hand playfully.

"You have to wait, Mrs. Porter." I give her a quick kiss on the lips, and when she starts to walk away from me, I smack her ass.

"Keep your hands to yourself, mister. If I don't get brownies, you don't get my ass." She wiggles her fine ass out of the kitchen, and I shake my head at her.

After Avery checks on Zoey, she comes back to the kitchen, and I pull her into my arms.

"Thanks for all this." She waves her arm in the air. "I love you." She stands on her toes and pecks me on the mouth.

"And I love you. I just wanted you to be able to relax tonight and not worry about dinner."

"That sounds heavenly." She moans. "I didn't realize how bad I needed out of the house until I sat down in the coffeehouse without a baby attached to me." She laughs. "Although, I missed her like crazy."

"I figured you did when you called me fifteen minutes after you left," I say teasingly.

She sniggers. "I know, I'm pathetic. It's just that she's been with me for the last nine months, it was kind of weird."

"You're not pathetic. You're a wonderful mother. You know that?" I run my hand through her hair as I still hold her in my arms.

"And you're a wonderful father. I couldn't do this parenting thing without you."

"Well, no. You couldn't get yourself knocked up."

"Evan!" She slaps my chest as she laughs.

"I can't wait to practice knocking you up again." I wiggle my eyebrows at her.

"Sorry. You've got four more weeks. Not that I'm counting or anything."

Apparently, my girl is just as anxious to have sex again as I am.

❧ 13 ❧

EVAN

"You sure you don't want me to stay home a couple more days?" I ask as I look at my wife through the bathroom mirror.

"Ev, stop. We'll be just fine. I'm a kick-ass mom, remember?" She winks at me.

"Yes, you are." I walk back to the bedroom and peck her on the lips, but then take the kiss deeper. "Only twenty-six more days until I get to have my wicked way with you again," I say as I pull away from our kiss and rub her nipple through her see-through maternity nightgown. I don't care what she's wearing. Or not wearing. She's always sexy as hell.

"Those are off limits too!" She swats at my hand. "Unless you want me leaking milk all over your clean suit."

"Fine, but soon, they're going to be all mine again."

She rolls her eyes before turning from me. "Not if you keep knocking me up."

"We'll see!" I holler as I walk down the hallway.

She follows after me.

I gently grab her face. "I'll miss you today, but next week, I get you all to myself." I give her a passionate kiss but then reluctantly pull away.

"Have a good day." She wraps her arms around me for one last hug before I walk out the door.

"Lock up behind me," I say as I pull the door open, and she gives me a mock salute. "I'm glad that motherhood hasn't made you less of a smartass, Av." I smirk.

"Nope. It'll take more than some poopy diapers and spit up to stop me."

TODAY HAS BEEN an absolute day from hell and can't seem to end fast enough. I'm sure the fact that I'm missing both my girls like crazy, doesn't help. With Christmas only a week away, the office is extra busy, and everyone seems to be in a piss-poor mood.

"Hey, man. Glad to have you back." Malcom pats me on the back as he reaches around me to grab a coffee mug. As much of an arrogant asshole he can be at times, he's really a genuine guy.

"Hey. Can't say I'm thrilled about being here. Would much rather be home with my wife and daughter."

"Yeah, I'm sure. How's the baby?" He stirs sugar into his black coffee.

"She's perfect." I smile, and I know I look like an idiot, but being a dad has done that to me.

"Dude, I can't believe you have a kid."

"Honestly, me neither. But I fucking love it."

"I will definitely never be in your shoes, but I'm happy

for you." He slaps me on the back again and starts to walk away.

"You don't know that. You just need to find the right woman to help settle your ass down first." I laugh at him.

"That won't happen either." He leaves the kitchen, and I'm left alone again.

I'm sick of being in my office, so I take a seat at the table and pull my phone out to send Avery a quick text.

Me: Hey, baby momma. Miss you and the princess today.

I know she'll scold me for calling her that as usual, but I love her fiery side. Although, I wish I could see her fiery side in the bedroom. Damn, I'm getting hard just thinking about her. I feel like a selfish prick since she just gave birth to our daughter, but I'm only a man. A very needy man.

I'm scrolling through my emails on my phone when a text from her comes through.

Avery: You better be good, mister. We miss you too and can't wait to see you in a few hours.
Me: What if I'm not good? Will you punish me?

I really shouldn't be texting her like this at work because it'll be near impossible to cover my hard-on when I walk back to my office.

Avery: Sorry... twenty-six more days, remember?

How could I possibly forget? All I know is that I need to find a babysitter for that night so we don't have any interruptions. I'm sure she'll argue with me about that, but she'll have to get over it.

Evan: Damn woman. You have a dirty mind. I wasn't talking about sex.

I chuckle to myself as I put my phone in my suit jacket pocket and walk to the sink to empty and wash out my mug.

I head toward my office, but before I make it to the door, I see Mallory walking out of Flynn's office.

"Hey, Mr. Porter," she says once she notices me.

"Mallory, I've told you before. Just call me Evan. I feel old when you call me that." I try to be funny, but I'm really not in the mood.

"You're not that old." She giggles. *Well, isn't that sweet?*

"Uh, thanks. I think." I laugh. "Did you need something?"

"No." She giggles again.

I turn toward my office to get back to work. "Okay, well, let me know if you need anything for the Ames case. I know it's going to be a messy one."

"Yeah, sure thing." She closes the door to her small office.

Mallory has been helping me do some research for a tricky case that Flynn put me on the week before I took off. I had some work I had to do at home to keep up with it, but thankfully, for the most part, the two of them took care of things while I was gone.

I plop down in my chair and rub my face with my

hands. I'm exhausted and can feel a migraine coming on. I really don't want to feel like shit when I go home tonight. I'm hoping to cook for Avery again, although I wouldn't be surprised if she took it upon herself.

Avery and I have been through so much together since we started dating. It hasn't all been good, especially the death of my parents. But she's been right by my side the entire time. I hope to God we're able to have more children someday. We haven't talked much about it, but I'm not even sure she'd want to try again after all the struggles we had to get pregnant with Zoey. Maybe we can consider the adoption route again.

I make a few last phone calls and shoot off some emails for a meeting we have tomorrow afternoon. Flynn will be out of the office for the rest of the week, so he's put me in charge of it. I won't lie and say I don't get paid good to work for them, but if I got paid for all the shit I do around here, I could buy my wife a mansion.

I pack up my briefcase with the few files I'll need to work on tonight once Avery and the baby are in bed. I hate taking work home with me, but unfortunately, that comes with the job.

When I walk to the front of the building, I hear Mallory's door shut, and I turn around.

"I didn't know you were still here, Mr. Porter." I don't know why, but when she calls me that, it causes the hair on my arms to stand up straight.

"I was just finishing up a few things."

Not feeling like dealing with anymore shit for the day, I head to the parking lot, ready to see my girls.

When I finally make it home and through the front door, I see my gorgeous wife dancing around the kitchen with Zoey strapped to her chest by some weird contraption she got at our baby shower. She likes it so she can get things done while she's holding her.

She doesn't notice me, so I continue letting her give me a show. She wiggles her ass and holds a spatula up to her mouth like a microphone as she sings to an N'Sync Christmas song. I've always teased her about her choice of music, but that's what makes me love her. She doesn't give a damn about what others think.

I'm not sure what she's making, but I don't care. I want more than anything to strip her out of her clothes and have my way with her. I'd leave the apron on though. It would be sexy as hell to fuck her with that thing on. But damn it... I can't be having those thoughts, because sex can't happen for another month. An excruciatingly, *long* month.

"Enjoying the show?" I was so lost in my lustful thoughts that I hadn't realized she was now looking at me.

I nod at her. "Very much." I take long, purposeful steps toward her and bring her into my arms, careful not to squish the baby. "I fucking missed you today." I run my hands through her hair before dipping my head down toward hers to take her lips into a heated kiss.

Once we finally come up for air, she smiles up at me. "I fucking missed you too. But we had a pretty good day on our own. Well, I guess we weren't completely on our own." She carefully lifts Zoey out of her sling and hands her to me before turning back toward the stove. She's stirring what appears to be melted chocolate.

"What do you mean?" I rub at Zoey's head and then

lean down to kiss it. She's sound asleep. I don't know how, but this little thing sleeps through everything.

"We went to my parents' so I could bake with my mom. Although, I ended up baking by myself while they watched Zo. Can't say I minded though."

My girl loves to bake. I've always thought she should open a bakery, but she had her mind set on being a designer. And she is damn good at her job.

"Did you bring any home for me?" I look around the kitchen and then spot the Christmas containers sitting on the counter. "Jackpot!" I open the top one and see sugar cookies. She makes these bad boys every year, and damn are they good.

"You're going to spoil your dinner," she says as she pulls a pan of something out of the oven.

"I thought you were baking. Did you make dinner too?"

"Yeah, I wanted to make a nice dinner for you after your first day back to work." She looks at me shyly, and it's fucking adorable.

"You're incredible. You know that?" I set Zoey down in her seat next to the table and then walk back to my wife. I trail kisses along her neck and then remember that I need to keep this PG or I'm going to have to take a cold shower to get rid of the raging hard-on I'm sporting right now.

"You work hard for us. It's the least I can do." She gives me a quick kiss on the lips.

We both turn toward the baby when we hear her squealing in her seat.

"Will you change her diaper while I finish up here, and then I'll feed her?"

"Sure thing, beautiful." I kiss her on the cheek before

taking Zoey to the nursery. I'd never changed a diaper in my life prior to becoming a father and I'm still terrible at it, but I love that Avery doesn't care how much I screw up. I'll do anything for my girls, even if that includes changing the shitty diaper my daughter just graced me with.

❧ 14 ❧

AVERY

Zoey and I spent the afternoon at my parents' house. When we came home, I took a nap while she was sleeping. I keep forgetting that I still need to be resting and try not to overdo it. My doctor told me at my follow-up appointment the other day that just because I feel like I'm alright, doesn't mean I shouldn't be taking it easy. After all, I did just push a kid out of my vagina. Okay, he didn't say those exact words, but that was the gist of our conversation.

When I woke from my nap, Zoey was still sound asleep, so I decided to do some more baking. I hope Evan's office is in the mood for some goodies, because like it or not, they are getting a bunch tomorrow. I'll also take some by Kinsley in the morning. Carly keeps begging me to bring Zoey by the office.

"She ready to eat now that she's got a clean butt?" I laugh at Evan as he walks back into the kitchen with Zo. I knew she had left a little present in her diaper, but I don't think he realized that when he willingly took her to the nursery.

"You knew, didn't you?" He sets Zoey back in the bouncy chair and then makes his way to the stove where I'm mixing cereal into the melted chocolate and butterscotch to make scotcharoos. I swear I'm going to gain more weight eating all this junk than I did being pregnant.

"I don't know what you're talking about," I say as I bat my eyes at him.

"Avery Porter, you are an evil, evil woman. You know that?" He spanks my ass before walking out of the room.

"You love me though!" I holler at him.

"Yes, I do." He turns and winks at me.

"Hey, can you get my Christmas stuff down from the attic so I can decorate tonight?"

He raises his eyebrows at me. "You want to do all that tonight?"

"Well, yeah. Christmas is only eight days away." I know it's probably silly for me to even bother with it now, but I want to enjoy it for the little time I can.

"Sure, I'll go get it. But let me put it up. You need to relax. I know Dr. Cooper told you not to overwork yourself."

I sigh. "You're right. You put up the tree, and then I'll just decorate it. Sound good?"

"Yep."

Zoey starts to cry from across the room, reminding me that she still needs to eat. I don't know how women do it with multiple children. It's hard balancing everything with only one.

"Come see Momma, baby." I lift my sweet girl into my arms and then take her to the living room so I can sit in the recliner to feed her. She's a slow eater, so I like to get comfortable. Sitting on a hard ass chair in the kitchen is definitely out of the question.

I unbutton my long-sleeved denim shirt I paired with black leggings. Then I open my maternity bra before Zoey has a conniption because I'm not going fast enough for her liking.

"I'm coming." I place my nipple into her mouth and then relax into the chair. It usually takes her a good forty-five minutes to eat.

"Here's all eighteen totes," my husband says as he sets my Christmas tubs on the floor.

"Oh, don't be dramatic. There's only six." As much as I love Christmas, I am kind of surprised by the fact that I don't have more decorations. Although, they do cover the entire house.

He grins at me and then leans down to kiss me. "You two are beautiful, you know that?"

"And you are a sweet talker. You know that?" I smile up at him.

"I try my best. Where would you like the tree this year? By the front window again?"

"Yeah, that's perfect."

Evan finishes putting the tree up, and I lay Zoey in her seat.

"Thanks, baby." I wrap my arms around his middle as he still faces the tree.

"Welcome, beautiful. I'll help you decorate so you can get done faster." He opens the tote labeled Christmas ornaments and starts to put them on the tree.

"Hold on. We need to put the lights on first."

This is the worst part of decorating, but thankfully, I

put them all neatly in the box last year when I took everything down. Tangled-up lights are a true nightmare, and nothing else could put me in a worse mood.

"When we're finished, we can eat and then have some cookies."

"Let's get done fast then. I'm dying for some more of those sugar cookies." I smile at him. Evan is a very career-driven man who takes his job seriously, but when he's home with me, I get to see a side of him that many don't get to.

We quickly finish the tree and then both step back to admire our work.

"It's gorgeous."

"Yes, you are." I turn to him, and he's eying me with lust.

"You always know what to say to me." I hug his middle. Even when I'm feeling like the Marshmallow Man after having the baby, he still makes me feel like the most beautiful woman alive.

"Well, it's the truth." He kisses my temple. "Now, what's for dinner? I'm starving."

We enjoy a quiet dinner of meatloaf, mashed potatoes, and corn.

After we're finished eating and get all the dishes put in the dishwasher, Evan goes to the living room to start a fire. It doesn't get too cold in Phoenix in the winter, but it's still chilly out. Only in Arizona are there days where you have to run the AC and the heat in the same day.

I make us each a plate of cookies and then pour hot water into two mugs to make hot cocoa. I'm typically a coffee girl, but there's nothing like a good cup of cocoa with Christmas cookies.

"Here you go." I hand him a plate and his mug before returning to the kitchen for mine.

Once I have my cookies, I snuggle into his side and sigh in contentment as he wraps his arm around me.

We both stare at the tree in front of us. I think about how fun Zoey is going to be next year at Christmas. This year she won't have a clue as to what's going on, but I'm glad we'll get to spend the holiday with her. I can't wait to make memories with our sweet girl and the man sitting next to me.

"I love you, Avery Porter," Evan says, breaking the silence.

"I love you, Evan Porter. Thanks for being so wonderful to me."

He looks down at me with his handsome smile stretched across his face.

"I hope I always make you feel that way."

"You will, baby. I just know it."

15

EVAN

"I understand. Thank you for calling." I hit end on my phone and then throw my head back against my seat. *Fuck. Fuck. Fuck.*

I slam my hands down on the steering wheel, causing the horn to go off. I'm sure people are staring at me in the parking lot.

I'm sorry, Mr. Porter, but we found someone who is more qualified for this position.

I know I still have about five more months before I have to have something in place, but I'm already freaking the fuck out. How can I provide for my family without a goddamn job? I'm starting to think that Avery has way too much faith in me. I just hope I don't let her and our daughter down. There's nothing that busts a man's balls more than knowing he can't take care of what's his. Not that we won't be fine for a while, but the funds will eventually dry up. There's no way I'm depending on my wife and her job.

I pull out of the parking lot, but instead of going right,

I turn left toward Ryke's bar. I know that alcohol won't fix everything, but it sure as hell can't hurt right now.

"What up, man?" Ryke asks as soon as I take the stool at the end of the bar. I know I can't have more than a couple drinks or I'll have to walk home, but I need something to numb the shitstorm swirling in my brain right now.

I slam my hand on the bar, probably harder than necessary, but if Ryke notices, he doesn't let on.

"I desperately need a beer." I rub at my temples and throw my head back.

He looks at me questioningly. "Rough day?" He turns around and grabs a bottle of Corona out of a small fridge and then sets it on a napkin in front of me.

I chuckle. "You could say that."

He raises his eyebrows. "You wanna talk about it?"

"Oh, you know. Interviewed for a job and didn't fucking get it." I tip my head back and take a swig, not coming up for air until half the bottle is gone. I slam it on the bar and then wipe my face with the back of my hand. Real attractive. I know.

"Damn." He pauses. "Let me get you another."

I spend the next hour sulking at the bar while Ryke waits on other customers. Austin gives me a few more beers and a new guy, I don't recognize, gives me I don't know how many. Needless to say, I'm starting to feel the effects. I lay my head on the bar, starting to feel like shit because I don't typically drink like this. Call me a lightweight, or whatever, but I feel like I've been hit by a fucking train only to have it back up and hit me all over again.

"What the hell? How many drinks has he had?" I hear

Ryke behind me. He's clearly not asking me, so I keep my head down, ignoring him. My head is starting to pound, and I have a feeling that the room will spin if I sit up.

"I only gave him a few," Austin tells him. "He looked like he was having a shitty day. I was just trying to help."

I feel a whack on the back of my head. "Get your ass up. I'm taking you home."

I slowly look up and squint my eyes, because the light in here is killing me. I just want to go home and sleep the rest of the day away. Avery is going to kill me.

"Just what I want to do…" I stutter, "go home and face my wife after being told I didn't get the job." I lay my head back down before throwing up. I'm dizzy as shit.

The next thing I know, I'm laying in the back of Ryke's truck. If he doesn't stop hitting those damn bumps, I'm going to puke my brains out.

"We're here," he says as he unhooks his seat belt. He then turns to the backseat. "Dude, I hate to sound like a dick, but I don't think you give Avery enough credit." He shakes his head and then opens his door before opening mine.

I feel too sick to argue with him. If I were sober, I'd punch his stupid face.

"Thanks for bringing him home," Avery says as Ryke ushers me into the house. I stumble, hardly able to walk. I somehow make it to the couch before falling on my ass. "What the hell happened?" I hear the concern in her voice.

"Once he sobers up, you need to talk to him. Are you okay if I get back to the bar?" he asks before leaving the room. They're talking as if I'm not in here with them. Although, I'm not sure I'd be able to respond if they tried talking to me.

She sighs. "Yeah, we're fine. Thanks again."

I hear his footsteps in the hallway, and in the next second, the front door slams shut.

"You wanna tell me what the hell is going on?"

I peek one eye open, but the room is spinning like I'm on a freaking merry-go-round. I hated those things as a kid, and I can't say I'd enjoy it any better today.

I carefully push myself up, propping my back up against the arm of the couch.

Avery stands with her hands on her hips.

I clear my throat. "I didn't get the job," I mumble, and part of me hopes she didn't hear me. I really don't feel like having this discussion right now.

I chance a look up at her and see the disappointment etched on her face. I'm not sure if she's disappointed because I didn't get the job, or because I'm drunk off my ass at eight-thirty in the evening.

She doesn't say anything right away, which scares me. I love my wife, but I know that the silent treatment from her is far worse than any time she's ever yelled at me.

"That's what this is all about?" She sounds exasperated.

I rub my face with my hands and throw my head back. Again, not the smartest idea because I'm one wrong move away from losing everything I've eaten today all over the living room rug. Then she'll be even more pissed off at me.

"I've spent the last three hours worrying about you, because you didn't get a fucking job?" She laughs manically, which is not a pleasant laugh. If I didn't think I'd pass out when I got up, I'd run, far, far away from her.

"Av, if I don't have a job, we're screwed."

I don't think she's heard me at first, until I hear her

sigh, and then she stomps down the hallway and then slams our bedroom door. *What the hell did I do?*

16

AVERY

I've been staring at the ceiling for an hour. After Evan came home drunk off his ass last night, I couldn't look at him. I understand that he's stressed about finding a new job, but it pisses me off that he thought I'd be that upset about him not getting the position at Reynolds & Sons. I'll be going back to work in a few weeks, so it's not like we'll be completely without. Plus, we've been smart about saving since we got married. But he's too bull-headed to let anyone take care of him. He'll be at Howser & Bowman for another five months anyway. I love that man, but he's starting to act like his father. If he knew I thought that, he'd be quick to pull his head out of his ass.

I sigh and throw the blankets off. I was hoping to fall back to sleep for a bit before Zoey wakes again, but my mind is spinning.

I look over at the monitor that sits on the side table next to our bed, and she's still snoozing away, making adorable little noises with her mouth. God, I love that little girl and her stubborn ass daddy. I know I shouldn't be too upset with him, but he can't act like this.

I go to the bathroom to relieve myself and brush my teeth and then slip my robe on. As I'm heading to the kitchen, I hear Evan snoring from the couch. I start some coffee, knowing he'll need caffeine once he rejoins the land of the living. He's been out cold since soon after he got home last night.

Once the pot is finally done brewing, I grab my favorite mug and pour a cup and add a little bit of cream. I lean up against the counter and roll my neck side to side. There are so many emotions running through me at the moment, but I think that sadness overrules the rest. I'm sad because Evan and I never let shit like this get to us. We never let it come between us, and I feel like that's what happened last night. Don't get me wrong. We've had our fair share of arguments over the years, but I think this was only the second time we slept apart by choice. The night before our wedding, my mother said to me, *"Never go to bed angry at each other."* And that has always been something I've thought about, especially since Sierra lost Miles.

"Hey." I look up at the sound of Evan's gravelly voice, and he looks worse than I feel.

"Hey. I'll get you coffee and a couple of ibuprofen." I turn to get him what he needs, but I'm halted when I feel him wrap his arms around my waist.

"Av, I'm fine." He presses his face into my hair, and I hear him inhale. He's always loved the smell of my shampoo. Crazy man.

I sigh and then turn toward him.

"Look, I'm sorry for fucking up last night." I hate seeing him look so defeated. Since being married to him,

I've started to better understand the term soul mates. When he hurts, it feels like someone is reaching inside of me and crushing my soul with their bare hands.

I don't answer him with words, but instead wrap my arms around his waist, and I immediately feel him relax.

"I shouldn't have been so dumb and come home like that. It was stupid, especially with Zo here."

I look up at him.

"She's fine." I give him a small smile as I rub at the day-old scruff on his face. "But next time, just talk to me, babe. I know you're disappointed about not getting the job, but it's okay. Something will come through for you." He starts to interrupt, but I put my finger to his mouth. "I don't want to hear any more. Okay? I know you're worried, but for now, you have a job."

He nods. "How the hell did I get so lucky?"

I stand on my toes and kiss his cheek. "I'm the lucky one. Now, do you want some coffee?"

"Sure, but why don't you go take a shower and get our girl dressed. I want to take my wife out for breakfast."

I frown because we've never taken Zoey out, besides to my parents' house and the pediatrician.

"Zo will be fine." Damn, how can this man always read my mind? *Soul mates.*

I sag into him and nod. "Okay, I'll go shower. Will you listen for her?"

"Of course." He kisses the top of my head before I head to the bathroom.

FINALLY, an hour and a half later, we are sitting at Rise 'N

Shine, our favorite breakfast diner. Evan had to remind me that we were only going to be out for an hour, not a week, when I started packing Zoey's diaper bag.

"What can I get you two?" an older lady with gray hair up in a messy bun asks.

"I'll take a decaf and water," I say, and Evan orders the same, minus the decaf. I've already exceeded my caffeine limit for the day.

Once our waitress walks away, Evan reaches across the table and grabs my hands.

"I really am sorry."

I smile at him. "I know you are. I'll tell you what. Why don't we go home when we're done eating and I'll help you look online for job openings?"

"I'll handle it." He sags back in his seat.

"Why do you have to handle it on your own? You don't have to do everything yourself."

"I'm supposed to take care of you, Avery. Not the other way around," he mumbles.

I stand from my side of the booth and slide into his and wrap my arms around him. I'm sure we look ridiculous, but frankly, I don't care. I want him to know how serious I am. He's told me several times how his father always thought he had to do everything himself. And he taught him that he shouldn't rely on other people. Well, damn it, I don't give a shit what he thought. I want to help my husband, so I am.

"You do take care of me. Of *us*, but it's okay to need help sometimes. I know this is really hurting your ego right now, but please just let me in. Don't shut me out, okay?"

He pulls me into his side. "God, I fucking love you," he whispers into my ear.

"And I fucking love you."

I go back to my side of the table so I can be next to Zoey if she needs me, and then we enjoy our breakfast of scrambled eggs and Belgian waffles. This place has the best waffles in Phoenix.

Zoey continues to sleep, so we spend the next hour laughing and chatting about nothing and everything. I love how we can still discover new things about each other.

"I think I'll go into work this afternoon for a few hours," he says before taking a sip from his mug.

I nod. "Yeah, that's probably a good idea. I called Flynn last night to let him know you probably wouldn't be in this morning."

He smiles and then lightly kicks me under the table. "Thanks for that."

"We're a team. You take care of me, but I want to do the same for you." I shake my head. "God, I sound like a cheesy Hallmark card."

He chuckles. "Well, you're my cheesy Hallmark card."

I already feel better after spending the morning out with him.

17

EVAN

"Thank you all for taking time out of your busy holiday schedules to join us tonight. It has been crazy around here for the last month or so, and I know you all could use a break and maybe a nice drink." Flynn jokes as he holds his wine glass in the air.

I didn't want to leave Avery and Zoey tonight to come to this boring as hell Christmas party for work, but I felt like it probably wouldn't look good if one of their top lawyers didn't show up. There's around forty people here between everyone from both offices and their significant others. Only a few of us are here alone, which makes me not want to be here even more. Avery has always come with me in past years. Having her on my arm at least made it tolerable.

The banquet hall Howser & Bowman rented out for the occasion is decked out with Christmas decorations. Each large table that seats ten people is covered with gold tablecloths and in the center sits a clear vase with a red candle in it. Garland wraps around the banister leading up to the next level and white lights are strung from the ceiling, which give the room an inviting feel with the overhead lights turned down. In the center of the room sits a large, white tree covered with more white lights and red and green ornaments.

"Evan." Flynn greets me.

"Hey, Flynn. This is a nice party you've got here." I wave my hand around the room. "Avery told me to tell you she's sorry she couldn't be here tonight. She didn't want to leave the baby." Which isn't a complete lie, but she had offered to come tonight. I told her I'd rather her just stay with our daughter. I'm hoping it gives me an excuse to bail early.

"Please tell her not to be sorry."

"Thank you, sir." I take a swig from my bottle, trying to fill the uncomfortable silence between us. It has been nothing but awkward around him since he told me about the firm closing.

"I wanted to talk to you about something." He looks around the room, seeming to make sure nobody else is within earshot.

"Sure. What's up?" I'm wondering what's so important that it can't wait until later.

"I got a call from the firm in Dallas today, and Gerald's partner has decided to retire earlier than he had originally planned. They're really interested in you."

"Okay?" I question, hoping I don't sound like an ass but wondering why he's telling me about this, after I already told him I wasn't interested.

The next words out of his mouth surprise me. "How would you feel about transferring? They'd pay for your moving fees and put you up in an apartment or hotel until you're able to find a new house." When I raise my eyebrows at him, he continues. "I know you said you didn't think Avery would want to move, but I think this could be really good for you. And you'd be a great addition to the firm."

I feel like I can't turn this opportunity down again, when I still haven't had any luck finding anything here.

"Can I talk to her before I give you an answer?"

"Yeah, sounds good. Don't take too long though because they need to know."

I nod, and he leaves me to my thoughts.

I spend the next hour pretending to enjoy myself as I roam around the room, talking to different people. I'm introduced to several I've never met. I hate these things with a strong passion, but when you work in one of the largest law firms in Phoenix, you're expected to attend any and all events like this. I've never quite understood the purpose other than to pull me away from other things I'd rather be doing. Tonight, that is spending time with my wife and newborn daughter.

My phone dings in my suit jacket, and when I pull it out, I see that it's a text from Avery. I smile like an idiot before opening it.

Avery: Hey, handsome. You enjoying yourself?

I chuckle before responding.

Me: No, this is boring as hell. I'd rather be at home with you and Zo.

I make my way toward the bathroom because I'm

feeling the repercussions of the two beers I've had tonight. I won't drink anymore since I have to drive home, but I had to have something to ease the pain of being here. Malcom somehow got out of coming tonight. *Shit head.*

Once I'm finished, I pull the door open and run smack dab into Mallory.

"Oh, hey, Mr. Porter." She gives me a half hug, which makes me uncomfortable. Tonight, she's wearing a low-cut green dress with black knee-length boots. Avery always complains that she's flirting with me, so I try to be careful with what I say to her. Apparently, I'm a dumbass and don't notice shit like that.

I decide not to correct her for calling me by my last name again. There's no point, since she doesn't listen anyway.

"Hey, Mallory. Are you enjoying yourself tonight?" I decide that since I'll most likely be stuck here a little longer, I might as well make a plate of food. Tonight, they went all out with several different types of sushi, fruit dishes, and a bunch of different desserts.

"I am. I've met a lot of great people too." She giggles and then takes a sip from her martini. "How are Avery and the baby?" She's only met Avery a few times.

"They're good."

She nods her head. "Please give her my best." She gives me a megawatt smile and then looks out at the crowd.

"Will do." I give her a small smile in return.

Without turning back to me, she says, "You know? There's a new bar in town. We could leave this shitty party and go have a drink, and no one would probably even notice we left."

I chuckle. "I think I'm going to head home, but try to have a good night."

"Oh, come on. Just one drink."

I laugh. "Thanks for the offer, but I'm pretty tired."

"Oh, okay. See you Monday."

I spot Flynn across the room talking and decide not to interrupt him, but to take this as my opportunity to leave. I'm dying to get home to my wife.

BY THE TIME I finally make it home, the house is dark other than the lights glowing on the Christmas tree. I slip my shoes off at the door and then make my way to the kitchen to grab a glass of water as I undo my tie. I hate wearing the damn things.

"Hey." I turn toward the sound of my wife's sweet voice, and the vision of her steals my breath.

"Hey, beautiful." I set my glass in the sink and then wrap my arms around her. "How was your night?"

She smiles up at me. "It was good. Zo went down a couple hours ago, and I've just been reading." She snuggles into my chest. "How was the party?"

I moan, "Horrible." I hear her laugh into my chest.

"I'm sorry, baby. I know you hate those things, but at least you showed up so nobody can complain now."

"True." I pause. "I almost forgot. Flynn told me about a job in Dallas tonight."

I feel her stiffen in my arms. *Fuck, I didn't think that through very well.*

"What?" she rasps out as she looks up at me, and I know that I have to turn it down, *again*.

"Don't worry. I'll tell him no. There's no way we could leave Arizona. We just had a baby and all our family and friends are here." I feel bad for lying, but there's no way I can tell her that I think we need to make this move. Her and Zoey come first, but it looks like I'll be searching harder now for something here. "I'll find something here." I kiss the top of her head.

I feel her sag into me as she relaxes.

"I made a list of openings I found online tonight while you were gone."

"Great." I give her a weak smile. "I'll have a look."

"Let's go get Daddy." I hear Avery say while I still have my eyes closed. It's Christmas morning, and I'm eager to spend the day with my girls. We spent yesterday with her family and Ryke and Claire, but today, we plan to have a low-key day at home.

I peek one of my eyes open. "Merry Christmas," I croak out, still half asleep. I sit up with my back propped against the headboard and reach for Zoey. "Come see Daddy, baby girl."

"Merry Christmas." My wife places a gentle kiss on the top of my head before handing me our daughter.

I cradle her in my arms as Avery rounds the bed to join me under the blankets. It's a bit chilly in the house this morning. She snuggles into me, and I drape my free arm around her.

"Merry Christmas, princess. What did Santa bring you this year?" I hear Avery giggle beside me.

"I don't think she cares about Santa yet."

I gasp in mock horror. "What? Doesn't care about

Santa?" I look down at Zoey. "That's not true, is it Zo? Your momma has lost her mind."

She playfully swats at my naked chest, and I grab her hand.

"I'm gonna go make some coffee and breakfast."

"Sounds good. We'll be out soon."

A year ago, our Christmas wasn't as enjoyable as this one. Don't get me wrong. We were happy as a couple. Head-over-heels happy, but we had once again gotten a negative pregnancy test the night before. Avery had cried herself to sleep that night and told me she didn't want to try again. The heartache was becoming too much for her. It was for me as well. A few months later, we started the adoption process, but then soon after found out we were expecting our own child. We had considered continuing with the process, but we decided that another family should have the opportunity to have what we had wanted for so long.

I kiss her little head and then lift us from the bed.

"Come on, Zo. Let's go find your momma."

We get to the kitchen, and my gorgeous wife is dancing around the kitchen while she sings along to *Rocking Around the Christmas Tree*. She wiggles her ass to the music, and I'm starting to have very inappropriate thoughts. I walk out of the room so I can put Zoey in her swing and then make my way back to the kitchen.

She doesn't hear me as I approach her and grab her hips. She jumps at first but then settles into my arms.

"You're teasing me." I nibble at her earlobe and then kiss along her neck.

She turns in my arms so she can look up at me.

"Whatever do you mean?" She bats her eyes at me and

then turns back toward the stove where she's scrambling eggs in one pan and frying bacon in another.

I get close to her ear.

"You know exactly what I'm talking about. I can't fuck you for a month, but I'm about to take you back to bed so you can pleasure me." I see the hair on her bare arms stand at attention, and I know I'm affecting her as much as she is me.

"You're an ass." She moans as she leans into my chest.

"No. You're the one teasing me over here by looking all sexy." I run my hands up and down her sides. "I'm trying to be a gentleman, but I'm just a man, Av. A man who is starving for his wife."

Despite my raging hard-on, I walk away from her, leaving her panting.

"Asshole!" she hollers at me, and I chuckle.

Damn. I'm in desperate need of a cold shower.

We spend the morning eating breakfast and then exchanging the gifts we got for each other. I got her a gift card to get a massage and her nails done. She got me the new Star Wars DVD and a dress shirt I had mentioned I liked when we were at the mall.

Now, we're sitting on the couch with all the lights in the house off but the Christmas tree and the glow from the fireplace. Above it hangs three stockings. The little pink one with glitter between our larger two.

"I'm glad we stayed home today," Avery says as she sips on her hot cocoa. I'm not sure how she's able to drink it with the marshmallows practically flowing over the side of the mug.

"Me too. I like being home with my favorite girls." She sets the mug on the coffee table and then snuggles further into me. We sit in silence as we watch Zoey sway back and forth in her swing across from us. She's been out for the last couple hours. She'll most likely wake soon wanting to eat.

Besides the crackle of the fire and the Christmas music softly playing, the room is silent until she surprises me with her next words.

"I think I want to wait until March to go back to work." I turn toward her, thinking maybe I heard her wrong.

"What?" I know there's shock in my voice, but she has been adamant about going back to work as soon as her maternity leave is up.

"Yeah. I talked to Mr. Kinsley the other day when me and Zo went to visit, and he said it would be okay if I took some more time off."

"That's great." I wrap her in both my arms as I nuzzle my nose into her hair, inhaling her intoxicating scent.

I'd love more than anything for her to not go back at all, but this will have to do for now.

"Want to watch a movie or something?" she asks as she kisses my cheek.

"Sure. I'll go pop some popcorn and cut up some summer sausage and cheese." I stand from the couch.

"Thanks." She starts flipping through Netflix.

I go to the kitchen and start making popcorn on the stove. I could just throw a bag in the microwave, but it'll taste better this way. I then cut up some sausage and cheese. This was a Christmas snack me and Claire grew up on, and Avery enjoys it too.

Once I'm finished, I bring the big bowl and two plates into the living room and set them on the table before returning to the kitchen for my beer and sparkling grape juice for Avery. She's never been a huge drinker, so I don't think she's missed it much since being pregnant and having Zoey.

"Milady." I hand her a plate and lean back into the couch as I dig into my own. "What movie did you decide on?"

"Miracle on 34th Street. That okay?" I smile and nod at her. My girl loves Christmas movies. I was never a fan of this movie, but if it makes her happy, I'll watch it.

We spend the next hour and a half watching the movie, only being interrupted when Avery had to feed Zoey, but she went back to sleep quickly.

She takes her to the nursery to change her diaper and clothes and then puts her in her crib. I stand at the doorway, watching my wife with our daughter, and I know I'll never get sick of watching them together.

"Ready for bed?" she whispers as she stands on her toes to kiss me on the mouth.

"Yeah." I grab her hand and walk her to our room.

❧ 19 ❧

AVERY

"Hey, you doing alright?" Evan reaches over the gearshift and grabs my bouncing knee.

"Yeah, I'm sorry. I really am glad to get away tonight. I just miss her." I hate that I'm ruining our time away, but this will be the longest I've ever been away from my baby.

He moves his hand from my leg to the back of my neck and squeezes.

"You're a good mother, but she's in good hands for the night." He removes his hand so he can use it to drive, but then continues. "How about we see how tonight goes? If you want to cancel our plans for the morning, we'll drive home early instead of hiking."

This causes the unshed tears to start falling. I've never been super hormonal, but I've definitely been feeling it lately. I guess I did just have a baby two months ago, but still. I'm not used to these mood swings. And to top it off, my husband is being way too sweet to me about this. If I'm being honest, I'm starting to get on my own nerves.

I shake my head even though he's looking at the road.

"No, I want to spend time away with you. I promise I won't ruin this for you." I turn toward the window, trying to gather myself.

A few weeks ago, Evan planned a getaway for us in Sedona. It's only a two-hour drive from Phoenix, so if we need to get back to Zoey, it won't be difficult. Today is Valentine's Day, so we used this as an opportunity to have some alone time before I go back to work in a couple weeks. After Christmas, I informed Mr. Kinsley that I was going to take him up on his offer of extending my leave, so I could spend some more time at home with Evan and Zo. I'm so glad I did because I'm not ready to go back yet.

Not only is it Valentine's Day, but we will hopefully be sleeping together for the first time since the baby was born. My doctor had said we only needed to wait six weeks, but as anxious as Evan was, he told me he wanted to wait to make sure he didn't hurt me. I'll admit I was a little frustrated at first, but if I'm being honest, I wasn't ready yet anyway. I had no idea how much having a baby could affect your body, even after they come out.

We finally pull into a long drive that leads to the beautiful cabin we rented. The pictures Evan showed me online were amazing and had me even more excited about coming. The grass surrounding the house is emerald green, despite it being so cold up here. There's a log stairway going up to the cabin with a beautiful wrap-around porch that sits at the top. My weather app says it'll be chilly tomorrow morning, but I'm hoping to convince Evan to bundle up with me to sit outside for our coffee. It's absolutely tranquil out here. I've lived in the city my entire life, but I think I could get used to this.

"Ev, this place is gorgeous." I continue to stare out the

windshield in awe of our surroundings. The next cabin over is several yards away so we are pretty secluded. Privacy is not something we're used to living in Phoenix.

"You like it?" As soon as he parks, he looks over at me with his boyish smile, which has my heart thumping in my chest.

"Like it? Babe, I love it. Thank you." I throw my arms around his neck and then lean back so I can kiss him. "I'm sorry for my little meltdown earlier. I really am glad to be here with you."

He rubs my face with his calloused hand. "I know you are. I'd be worried if you weren't a little nervous about leaving our baby. But you deserve this, Av. Okay?" He eyes me, I'm sure waiting for me to argue with him.

I nod. "Okay." I kiss him one last time before sliding back into my seat.

"Shall we?" he asks as he opens his door.

"Yes! I can't wait to see the inside."

He chuckles at me. "Okay, stay put." I love how after all these years he still opens doors for me. Ladies, chivalry really isn't dead.

Once he has our small suitcase out of the back, he opens my door for me, and I grab my purse off the floorboard.

This afternoon, it's pretty cool at only fifty degrees, so I'm dressed in my dark-washed skinny jeans, a long-sleeved thin T-shirt, and my warm teal Columbia jacket. My outfit is complete with my black Chuck Taylor's. My handsome guy is wearing his sexy form-fitting jeans with a black long-sleeved shirt.

We walk toward the cabin, and that's when I notice the creek along the side of it. The view is amazing with the tall mountains placed in the background. It really is surreal. I feel like I'm in a Thomas Kincaid painting.

The steps leading up to the house are steep, so I'm careful by grabbing the rail for support. The last thing I need is to lose my balance and fall down the stairs when we're who knows how far from the nearest hospital.

"Here, I'll take that." I grab for the suitcase as he reaches in his pocket for the key to the cabin.

He undoes the lock and then pushes the door open, and the sight before me is breathtaking. The place is a lot bigger than it looked from the outside with the gorgeous tall ceilings. It has an open floor plan, so we're able to see the entire house from where we stand at the front door. Straight ahead is a huge bay window with the most stunning view I've ever seen. I've never been a fan of not having blinds or curtains up, but we're pretty far away from anyone else, so it doesn't bother me. I bet the sunset is amazing to watch from here.

I look to the right and see the immaculate kitchen. The wood cabinets make it look cozy like the rest of the house, and the vintage hanging light that sits above the island, makes me want to run to the store just so I can cook something fancy in here.

Next, I notice the beautiful spacious living room with a large flat screen TV placed on the tall wall. This is unlike anywhere I've ever been. Claire and Ryke have a beautiful home in the mountains near Phoenix, but this place feels like Heaven. I'm a little sad that we'll only get to stay here one night.

"Let's go check the bedroom out." He wiggles his eyebrows, which has me giggling, but also makes me excited. We've both been waiting for this night for some time now, and I have a feeling that we won't be getting much sleep on the one night we probably should be trying to.

We climb the stairs and immediately at the top of them is a stunning king-sized bed with a beautiful log frame.

I plop down on the large bed and then notice the enormous master bathroom. From where I'm sitting, I can see a huge claw tub and two stainless steel sinks. I'm thinking a bath is sounding wonderful about now.

"What do you think?" Evan asks as he puts the suitcase on the bed and unzips it, looking for something.

"This place is amazing, Ev. I wish we could stay longer."

I look up at him and see the surprise on his face, but then it disappears in the next instant. I'm sure he's shocked to hear that I'm not as anxious to get home now that we're here.

"We'll come back, soon." He kisses the top of my head. "But, for now, shall we try out the tub?" He asks, and I reach my hand out for him.

"Why yes, we should."

❦ 20 ❧

EVAN

I was surprised when Avery agreed to go away with me for the night. Malcom's uncle owns this cabin and gave me a pretty good deal on it. We've visited Sedona, but never have stayed overnight before now.

I start stripping out of my clothes after turning on the tub faucet, but then look toward my wife who is still fully dressed. I raise my eyebrows at her.

"Av? You forget how to undress?"

She looks at me shyly, and I'm wondering if she's having second thoughts about having sex tonight. I'll admit, I'm more than fucking ready for this, but if she's not, I won't be a dickhead and push her.

She slowly starts to pull her clothes off, and once her shirt is on the floor, I notice that she's trying to cover her stomach with her arms. Suddenly, it dawns on me what's going on.

I take the few steps toward her and pull her arms down to her sides.

"Don't hide from me, beautiful," I whisper into her ear.

"You are stunning. Possibly even more stunning now since carrying my child." I rub at her stomach, which became a habit of mine while she was pregnant. I hate that she's feeling insecure right now. Sure, we've been naked together since she had Zoey, but I think that in her mind this is different, and she worries that I'll be disappointed with how she looks.

"Okay," she says softly.

I smile, happy with her response, and then reach around her back to unhook her black lace bra. It makes her perky tits look amazing, but right now, I need them out of their confines.

Once she's uncovered, I palm both of her breasts with my large hands and then bend to take one of her nipples into my mouth. I hear her moan as I run my tongue in circles around it and then grab the twin nipple and start to twist it between my thumb and finger.

"Don't stop." She pulls at my hair, and I'm glad to see that my confident wife is back. The pressure she's causing on my head is causing my dick to pulse through my boxers. It's begging to come out, so I pull away from her just long enough to take them off.

"Off." I demand as I start to pull at her pants. Any other time I'd try to help her out of them, but right now, I don't have the patience for that. I want to make tonight special for her, but I don't know how long I'm going to last.

Without saying a word, she unbuttons her jeans and slides them seductively down her legs. A groan slips through the back of my throat when I see the matching black lace panties.

"Did you buy these for me?" I whisper into her ear as I run my thumb along the top of her panties.

"Yes." She pants, and I can tell that my girl isn't going to last long either. That's okay. We have all night.

I drag them down her gorgeous body and then lift her into my arms. Her legs instinctively wrap around me. My throbbing cock pokes her flat stomach, but I don't care. She needs to know how much I want her right now. I always fucking want her.

I carefully lower us into the tub, and she stays facing toward me as we sit. Once I have us situated, I slide my hand between our bodies and run my finger through her slick folds. She throws her head back, and it's truly a miracle that I haven't lost my damn mind yet.

"Look at me, Av." She looks up at me with desire in her eyes. She's so goddamned beautiful, and I cannot wait to be inside of her.

I grab the soap off the ledge of the tub and squirt some into my hand before using it to massage her body with the vanilla scent. I grab both of her breasts in my hands, and she moans as she rubs her wetness along my throbbing hardness. I wasn't planning on fucking her in the tub tonight, but this has quickly escalated out of my control. I do my best to rinse her off by cupping water in my hands and splashing it on her body. I then swat at her ass, motioning for her to stand.

"Up." I can't think of more than one-word phrases right now.

She looks at me questioningly, but then complies as she reaches for the towel on the counter. I stand and then help her dry off before grabbing my own.

I grab her hand to help her out and then lift her into

my arms before making our way back to the bedroom.

"You okay?" I ask as I set her on the bed and then continue to dry her off. She hasn't said much so I want to make sure I'm not pushing her to do something she's not ready for yet. I know she wants this, but I don't want to hurt her.

"I'm more than okay." She rubs her soft hand along the short scruff on my face.

I lean down to kiss her before pulling the towel from her beautiful body.

"Lay back." I pull my own towel off and then drape my body over hers. She's shivering from the change in temperature, so I grab the blanket at the foot of the bed to cover us with.

I lift up slightly so I can see her better. "I love you, beautiful." I then devour her mouth in a searing kiss. I feel her hand slide between our bodies, and in the next instant, she has her tiny hand wrapped around my dick and fuck if it doesn't feel amazing.

I throw my head back.

"Av, if you keep that up, I'm going to make a mess on your hand, and I really want to come inside your warm pussy."

I hear her gasp beneath me.

"What are you waiting for then?" Her hand leaves my shaft and then both hands rub along the sides of my face before she brings her head up to kiss me again.

"You promise me you're ready for this?" I want to be sure because I'd rather die than cause her pain.

"More than ready."

"Okay. Tell me if I'm hurting you."

She nods, and that's all the answer I need before I'm

sinking into her warmth.

I look down at her to make sure I'm not hurting her, but if the look of desire etched on her face means anything, she's enjoying this just as much as I am.

I start out slow but then can't hold back any longer, my movements become quicker as I pump in and out of her. She rises off the bed the best she can to meet me thrust for thrust, and I know that there's no way in hell that I'm going to last much longer.

"Ahh!" my girl hollers underneath me, and I feel her pulsing around me. In the next second, I'm right behind her as I pound one last time into her, filling her with my warm seed.

I feel her quiver as my own spasms shoot through my body. I'm pretty sure that was the hardest I've ever come in my damn life.

Once we both come down from our highs, I roll over so I'm lying next to her.

"That was incredible," she says, out of breath, and I turn toward her voice.

"That was so incredible." I agree before giving her a kiss. "Stay put. I'll get a cloth to clean you up."

I'm hoping like hell that we can do that all over again in a bit.

I come back from the bathroom with a warm rag and gently clean between her legs. Seeing the wetness caused by our lovemaking, makes me not want to wait another minute to have her again, but I know I need to let her rest first.

Once she's cleaned off, I reach for her hand.

"Come on, beautiful. Let's go finish that bath we started."

❧ 21 ❧

AVERY

"You may have to roll me out of here." I pat my stomach.

"Ugh, same," Claire says as she sits across from me in the booth at Ryke's.

Zoey squeals beside me. When I look to my right, I see that she's now awake.

"Hi, baby girl." I lift her out of her seat and kiss her on the cheek.

"Here's Evan's burger and cheese curds." Ryke sets a to-go box on the table and then takes the seat next to his wife.

"Thanks, Ryke. You sure I don't owe you anything?"

"Nah, it's on the house." He winks at me and then kisses Claire on the cheek. "Kids being good for you today?" he asks as he grabs Aria's little hand in his. These big, burly, tattooed guys turn into softies with these little girls.

She covers her mouth with a yawn. "Yeah, I'm just

tired today. I really hope they both go down for a nap when we get home."

"You sure you don't mind running by the firm? You can just drop me off to get my car and I'll just take Zo."

"No, I want to see my brother, and I know Brady does too."

"Aunt Avvy, can we go see Eben?" Brady asks beside me. His little stutter makes my heart melt. This kid has me wrapped around his little finger, and he knows it.

"You bet, buddy."

"Alright, sweetheart, I've gotta get back to work, but I'll see you tonight." Ryke gives Claire a kiss on the mouth, and I look over to see Brady covering his eyes, and I chuckle.

"That's yucky!" he hollers, and the three of us roar with laughter.

"It is," I say. "Don't ever kiss girls, okay?"

He holds his hand out to me to shake. "Deal." This kid is freaking adorable.

We pack all three kids up and load them into Claire's van. That's one thing I don't think I'll ever do as a mom. I love my car too much and don't think I'd enjoy driving a minibus around town. Although, I don't think Claire imagined driving one either, but Ryke insisted she get it when she was pregnant with Aria.

"How's Evan's job search?" she asks as I'm reaching behind me, trying to get Zoey's pacifier back in her mouth.

I sigh. "Honestly, I don't know." I stare out the window.

"I love my brother, but he's a stubborn ass." She looks behind her, obviously making sure Brady didn't hear her.

I decide against correcting her, because every time I cuss in front of her kids, I get scolded. I guess my payback will be her teaching Zoey a thing or two we don't want her repeating.

I really can't disagree with her. He is stubborn.

Ten minutes later, we pull into the parking lot of Howser & Bowman. I grab Zoey's seat, and we all make our way to the red-bricked building.

"Hey Hilary," I greet the receptionist sitting behind the big oak desk.

"Hey, Avery. Oh, my goodness. Let me see that sweet baby!" In the next second, Zoey is completely unhooked from her car seat and in Hilary's arms. "Go on back. He was in a meeting with Flynn, but I think they're finished by now."

I thank her and head toward Evan's office. I was unaware that he had a meeting today. I wonder if it's about the office closing. If so, I'm guessing he won't be in a great mood now.

His door is open, so I don't bother knocking, but I suddenly have the urge to hit something, or rather, someone.

"Oh, hey, Avery," Mallory says as she pulls away from my husband, after stroking his arm with her long ass fingernails. If looks could kill, Barbie would be laid out on the floor right now.

The part that pisses me off the most? Evan doesn't even think anything of the fact that she was just touching him. God, I hate when I act like this.

He's on the phone, but looks up from his desk, clearly surprised that I'm here. Mallory heads for the door, so I lead the way, intending on saying something to her. She's chosen the wrong woman to mess with.

I take a deep, cleansing breath and then turn toward her. "I would appreciate if you would keep your hands off my husband."

She gasps dramatically and holds her chest, as if I've just offended her.

"Avery, I work with him, and I know he's a married man. I would *never* go after a married man."

A part of me doesn't believe her, and the other part feels like a bitch for assuming she would.

"Ignore her and go see Evan," Claire whispers into my ear. I don't know where she came from, but she probably just kept me from saying something else I'll regret later. I nod, even though I'm still a little pissed.

Mallory waves toward Evan's office. "He's on the phone with Dallas, trying to get everything finalized before your move." *What the hell is she talking about?*

I make my way past her, and Claire grabs my arm.

"Av, what the hell is she talking about?"

"I don't know. But will you go back out front with Zo?"

"Yeah, for sure. I'll wait for you." She pats my arm and then walks away.

I take a deep breath before walking back into his office.

When I enter, he looks up from his desk and then holds his finger up. I set his food on his desk and take one of the leather chairs across from him and try to school my features. I don't want him to know that Mallory got me riled up. He's obviously keeping something from me. What the hell did she mean by 'your move'?

After what feels like hours, he finally hangs up.

"Okay, Gerald, I'll be in touch with you soon. Thanks for calling."

He sets his phone on the receiver and then makes his way toward me. I stand, and he pulls me into a hug.

"This is a nice surprise." He kisses the top of my head. "Where's Zo?" he asks as he pulls away.

"She's out front with Hilary and Claire." I'm trying not to show any emotion in my voice, but I'm not sure how well I'm doing at succeeding.

He pulls away from me. "My sister is here? Oh, that's right. You girls were going to Ryke's for lunch today."

I nod. "Yeah, and then her and Brady wanted to see you, so we all came." I give him a tight smile.

He looks at me with concern on his face. "Av, what's wrong?"

I shake my head. "Nothing." I feel like I'm acting childish, but I'm afraid if I ask him what Mallory was talking about, I'm going to lose my shit in the middle of his office. I really don't feel like embarrassing myself in front of his co-workers today.

He grabs my face so I'm forced to look at him. "Don't lie to me." And then it's as if a switch flips, as he realizes what I'm upset about.

"You know, don't you?"

"Know what? No, I don't know anything, but Mallory said you were finalizing things for the move. What move, Evan?" By now, my tone has turned bitchy.

He sighs and pulls away from me before running his hand through his hair. That's always his telltale sign that he's stressed about something.

"Sit down." He points to the chair I had been sitting in earlier, but I don't sit.

"I don't need to sit down. Tell me what the hell is going on."

He throws his head back, obviously contemplating his next words. "Gerald Bowman wants to take me on as his partner in Dallas."

He wants to move to Dallas? We can't move. I thought he already turned them down? Everyone important to us is here.

"And you told him yes?" I ask slowly as I lower myself into a chair.

"No, but I have to give him an answer by the end of the week." He kneels between my legs and grabs my hands.

"Were you going to tell me about this? You told me that you turned them down."

He gives me a surprised look. "Of course, I was. I literally just got the offer this morning. Well, I guess this is the third offer I've gotten, but I turned him down before. I know you want to stay in Phoenix, but Av, we really need to do this. It would give us so many opportunities."

I stare at him with my mouth agape. My dream job is here. This wouldn't benefit me at all.

"What kind of opportunities does this give me? Huh?" My voice is getting louder at this point. "My job, family, *and* my friends are all here. Not in Dallas, Evan."

He doesn't respond right away.

"I want you to be able to stay home with Zo. Not leave her with some stranger every day. You know your parents aren't going to watch her forever."

I throw my hands up in exasperation. "Are you freaking

kidding me?" I shake my head. "We're in the twenty-first century. Women work, Evan, and kids go to daycare!" I yell, probably a little too loudly. I wouldn't be surprised if everyone out in the hall just heard my little outburst. I take a deep breath. "I'll let you eat and get back to work." I nod toward his food. "Claire and the kids are waiting for me."

I stand and turn toward the door, not wanting to discuss this any further right now.

"Av, we have to finish talking about this." He gives me a sad smile when I turn to look at him, and it makes my chest tighten. I hate fighting with him, but I'm angry. I'm angry that he's even considering moving us across the country. He moved away from his family, and it didn't bother him a bit, so there's no way he can understand why this would upset me.

I feel like if I stay here another minute, I'm going to say something I'll regret.

I shake my head. "Fine. You wanna talk about this now?" I point my finger at him. When he doesn't respond, I go on. "You go ahead and go to Dallas, but we won't be joining you." Shit. I should have left.

I see a flash of anger and hurt on his face.

"You've got to be fucking kidding me." He shakes his head. Two can play this game. If he wants to be controlling, I can be too.

"No. I'm not kidding, Evan. I have a job here and a newborn. I need to be here. Obviously, that job is more important to you than me and Zoey, so have at it." I wave my hand in the air. I know I'm acting like a crazy person now, but somehow, I can't bring myself to care.

"This is complete shit," he mumbles under his breath.

"I'm tired after being up all night with Zoey, so I really don't feel like dealing with this right now."

He walks toward me. "If you stayed home with our daughter, you wouldn't have the added stress of work and then you wouldn't be so tired."

"I don't know why you keep trying so hard to make me something I'm not, Evan, but I think it's time you stop. Maybe you should have married someone who wanted to be Betty Homemaker, but you knew that wasn't me. I love being a wife and mother, but that doesn't define who I am."

"I never said it did." He crosses his arms over his chest, and then he sighs. "Avery, I have to have a fucking job. If we stay here, I won't have a job, and I won't have a way to take care of my family."

I glare at him. "I have a damn job, *and* I gave you several websites to check out that had local opportunities. You're an attorney, Evan. You can find something here."

"I've worked for this company for seven years. I'm going to start at the bottom anywhere else."

I shake my head. "Whatever. I can't do this right now. If you want to go then fucking go."

Without letting him get another word in, I exit his office. I steel my spine before reaching Claire and Hilary. Nobody needs to know how upset I am right now, although I'm sure it's clearly written all over my face.

Just when I thought everything was perfect with my little family, something has to stand in the way. I just hope we're strong enough to fight it.

22

EVAN

Fuck. I have a feeling that taking flowers home to Avery, isn't going to make things better. So, I didn't even bother stopping this time.

After she left the firm this afternoon, I told Flynn that I would probably be turning down Gerald's offer. He then informed me that the finances were turning to shit at our office, so it would be in my best interest to take the Dallas job. He failed to mention that before. It looks like the doors may be closing much sooner than we had originally thought. That explains why he's been so adamant about me going. I can appreciate his willingness to help, but the asshole could have mentioned this sooner.

Avery was completely and utterly furious at me this afternoon. It pisses me off that Mallory had to be the one to tell her. She obviously didn't know what she was talking about, because she assumed that I had already taken the position. It's none of her damn business.

I pull into the driveway and see that she has the curtains pulled back on the living room windows. This time of day it's beautiful with the sun beaming through the glass. With the dark furniture and neutral colored walls, our house seems like a cave even during the day, if it's all closed off. I wouldn't be surprised if she's got a few windows open as well because it is unusually warm for this time of year.

I park in the garage next to Avery's car and then take a deep breath. It's not like I'm afraid of my wife, but I really don't like fighting with her, and I know that she's not thrilled about even entertaining the idea of moving.

"Hey, Av," I call out as I set my keys, phone, and brief-case on the hallway table.

"I'm in the kitchen," she hollers, and thankfully sounds like she's in an alright mood.

When I get back to the kitchen, she is standing at the stove stirring something in a big pot.

"Smells good in here. What are you making?" I ask as I wrap my arms around her. I feel her tense at my touch, which pisses me off, but I pretend not to notice. I really don't want to drive a wedge further between us.

"Goulash. It's my Grandma's recipe." She doesn't turn toward me, but I still drop a kiss on the side of her face before backing away.

"You've never made that before, have you?" I ask as I bend down to Zoey, who is sitting in her bouncy seat on the floor. "Hi, princess." I grab one of her tiny hands and bring it to my mouth. "Daddy missed you today."

"No, I was craving it though, so I got the recipe from my mom."

I sit at the table and watch her continue to work on dinner, and I have to wonder if or when she is going to bring up the Dallas topic again. I really just want her to understand where I'm coming from. If she's really not onboard after I finish talking to her tonight, I'll call Gerald first thing in the morning and turn him down. It's not worth risking my marriage for.

"What are you thinking about?" she asks with her back still toward me. I don't like that she won't look at me, but I'll let her have her way for now.

I stand and make my way toward her again.

"I'm thinking about the fact that I hate that you're mad at me." I wrap my arms around her waist.

She drops the wooden spoon she'd been using, and it crashes onto the stove. It sounds like something broke, but then I realize that there's just sauce all over the counter, stove, and the oven door. She doesn't seem to notice this though, because apparently, whatever she is about to say to me is more important.

She sighs heavily and then finally faces me, but I'm not sure if that's a good or bad thing.

"You hate that I'm mad at you, but yet you're still considering this huge ass move. How could you even decide something like this without talking to me first?"

I back away from her, wanting to give her a little space. And perhaps because I'm a little frightened of her right now.

"Av, I didn't decide anything yet, and I am talking to you about it. I just want you to try to understand why I think this is important."

She rolls her eyes in frustration. "Seriously? You don't think I know why this is important to you? You're just like your dad. All you care about is success." As soon as the words are out, her eyes nearly bulge out of her head, seeming to have surprised herself. Her hand goes to her mouth, as if she's willing them to go back where they came from.

Fuck, that hurt.

"Ev, I didn't mean it."

I shake my head as I start to leave the room. "How can you even say that? I'm nothing like my father, and you fucking know that." I growl.

I can tell that she's taken by surprise at my words.

Her defenses are going up now, and it's proven by what she says next. "If it's not important to you, then why do you want to rip me away from everything that's important to me?"

What the hell?

"Everything that's important to you?" By now, my voice is getting louder. I look toward Zoey to make sure I'm not upsetting her, but she seems oblivious to what's going on around her. "What about me, Avery? Your *husband.*" I spit the word husband out like it leaves a bad taste in my mouth.

"Whatever, I'm not doing this with you right now." She pushes past me, and I grab for her arm. "Let go of me." She hisses, and I can hear the venom laced in her voice. She's more pissed at me than before. I should have stayed at work.

"So, we're just not going to talk about this?" I say this in a calmer tone, hoping to get her to talk to me without fighting. But I have a feeling that tonight won't be the night for that.

She shakes her head. "No. I need to get Zoey changed and ready for bed. If you're hungry, dinner is done."

"Av, wait." She surprisingly stops in her tracks and turns back to me.

I exhale a heavy breath. "It looks like the firm might be closing sooner than we thought."

She raises her eyebrows at me. "What are you talking about?"

"Flynn told me today that the finances have gone to shit because a lot of our clients have already started looking at other firms. I don't even know if he can afford to employ me much longer."

She takes a seat at the table, looking defeated.

"Let me take this job, and you can find one there. Can you at least agree to that? If you insist on being so independent."

"Is that seriously what our marriage has come to, Evan? Just a big compromise?"

I take the seat across from her. "I don't know what else to do, but I know I can't do this without you."

"What about those other jobs I told you about?"

"Av, I already told you, I'd be starting at much lower pay. I really feel like we need to do this."

She rests her elbows on the table. "I have a job here. I could probably pick up more hours."

I hold my hand up, stopping her. "No."

"No?" She throws back at me with her eyebrows raised.

"I'm not letting you take care of me like that. End of discussion."

She slams her hand down on the table. Somehow, Zoey is now sound asleep beside us.

"We're supposed to be a fucking team, Evan."

"We are a team, but that doesn't mean I'm going to let you be the only one working."

"You know what? Just take the damn job."

"So, you're on board?" There's no way she'd agree to this so fast. She's as stubborn as they come.

She shakes her head. "Just take the damn job," she repeats as she goes to stand.

I grab her by the arm. "I need you to want this."

She gives a small manic laugh, and it's clear that she is *not* on board with this.

"Just do it. You don't give a fuck what I think or want anyway, so just do it."

Without letting me say another word, she lifts Zoey into her arms and leaves the room.

Fuck.

23

AVERY

I didn't sleep a freaking wink last night. Evan finally came to bed around midnight, and I pretended to be asleep. I feel like we are slowly drifting apart, and I don't know how to fix it. I know I could just cave and tell him that I'm happy to go to Dallas, but I'd be lying. I don't want to leave Phoenix. I guess I never thought about ever leaving, but now that he wants to, it scares the shit out of me. I know I upset him when I told him that everyone important to me was here. Of course, he's important to me, but he's not the only one.

"Wow, what's wrong with you?"

Leave it to Carly to not beat around the bush. She never worries about sparing my feelings, which is what I've always loved about her. But right now, it would be nice if she could sugarcoat things just this once.

I throw myself into my desk chair with a huff. Not wanting to be here this morning, but at least I'm not at home fighting with my husband. Although, the last twelve hours we were home together, we didn't speak at all. I'll admit that was my fault, but I'm just not ready to talk to him.

"You going to tell me what's going on, or are you going to make me guess? You look like someone pissed in your Cheerios this morning."

I chuckle. "I ate oatmeal."

I turn toward her as she's rolling her eyes. "Whatever. What the hell is wrong? You have a sexy as hell husband and an adorable baby. What could possibly be wrong in your life?"

When she says shit like that to me, I feel bad for acting like this. But this has put a damper on my perfect little life.

"Evan got offered a job in Dallas, and he's really considering taking it," I say this as quietly as I can because I don't need anyone in the office overhearing our conversation.

"What? You're leaving me?" She shakes her head. "No way. If I have to suffer in this hell, so do you."

"You're not helping," I mumble as I rub my temples with my fingers. I can feel a headache coming on.

In the next instance, she's up out of her chair.

"Come here." She pulls me to my feet. "You and that man are perfect together. Don't let something so silly, like moving across the country, ruin that."

I wipe at the tear that is now falling down my face and then sniff as I hug her back.

"I love him so much, but I can't imagine being away from my family. And what about Claire and the kids? She'll be crushed if we leave."

"You'll figure it out." She releases me so she can look at me. "I've never been in your shoes to give you advice on this, but I think you should hear Evan out. Maybe he's got a good reason for wanting to go."

I return to my chair and start up my computer. "He wants me to stay home with Zoey." I shake my head. "Car, I love being a mom, but I need to work."

"Why? Your man is telling you he wants you to say home with your child. Hell, I'd be all over that."

I snigger. "I love what I do." She raises her eyebrows at me. "I know, it sucks here sometimes, but this is truly my dream job, minus the shitty people we work for."

We both laugh, which thankfully lightens this too-heavy conversation.

"Your hot, sexy man loves you, but I think it drives him nuts with how freaking independent you are." It doesn't even phase me anymore when she refers to my husband as sexy. The girl has no filter, whatsoever.

"I'm not that bad, am I?" *God. What if I am?* I've always wanted to be able to take care of myself, but I'm acting the exact same way that I got upset at him for.

"Whatever you say, Momma."

"Hi, baby girl," I say to Zoey as I lift her from my dad's arms. "Were you good for Grams and Pops today?" I kiss her little cheeks and immediately feel relaxed. I don't know how she does it, but she always makes things better when I get the least bit stressed.

"She was very good. She watched the news with me, and then we ate pizza for lunch," my dad says as he stands from his recliner that has a nice indent in it because I'm sure that he spends most of his days in it, especially now that they watch Zo for us.

I smile at him as I roll my eyes.

"Pops is crazy, Zo," I say to her in a baby voice. "Hey, where's Mom?" I ask as I start packing up the diaper bag.

"I think she's on the phone with your sister in the kitchen, but she may be off now."

I nod. "Okay, I'm gonna go find her."

"Here, I'll watch her while you do that." I smile at him. I love how much he adores my daughter. He was and is an amazing dad to me and my sister. Somehow, he put up with three hormonal women while I was growing up. I know that was no small feat.

"Love you, Ains. Call me this week." My mom sets her phone down on the counter and then looks up at me. "Hey, Av. How was work?" My mom can read me almost as well as Evan can. As much as this woman makes me crazy at times, I need her right now. I know that she may not tell me what I want to hear, but maybe that's a good thing.

"It was okay." I smile at her. "Dad said Zo was good for you?" I lean on the counter, facing her.

"Of course, she was. Our granddaughter is perfect." She tilts her head to the side. "What's wrong, baby?"

I shake my head. "I don't know what to do," I try to speak quietly so my dad can't hear me. I don't know how he'll feel about us moving. I'm not ready to tell him.

"Come sit down." She walks to the kitchen table, so I follow.

"I feel like the worst wife." I put my head in my hands.

"For one, that's the furthest thing from the truth so get that out of your mind right now."

I nod, knowing that I can't argue with her.

"Evan was offered a partnership at a firm in Dallas, and he really wants to take it." When I look up at her, I see the pain on her face.

"Oh?" She pauses, waiting for my response. When I nod, she goes on, "That's great, isn't it?"

I rub my face with my hands. "I don't want to leave, and it caused us to have a huge fight last night."

She sighs. "Baby girl, that man loves you more than anything in the world."

"I know, but I just had a baby, and I need you guys." I sob, and at this point, I'd be surprised if my dad hasn't heard me from the other room.

"Av?" I look up at the sound of Evan's voice. I had no idea he was here.

I jump out of my seat and then into his arms.

"I'm going to give you two some alone time." My mom quickly leaves the room.

"I didn't know you were coming," I say into his shoulder as he rubs my back.

"I got done early today, so I thought I'd meet you here and say hi to your parents. Now I'm glad I did." He pulls away from me. "You okay?"

I nod against his chest. "I'm sorry," I say almost inaudibly. "I said some terrible things that I didn't mean."

"No." He shakes his head. "I'm sorry I even considered moving you away from here. I know your family is important to you. I called Gerald this morning and turned him down."

I gasp. "You did? I didn't know you were giving him an answer so soon."

"Well, I figured it was silly to leave him hanging if I knew we weren't going."

I put my head on his shoulder. "Call him back," I mumble into his ear. I'm not completely on board with this, but it's important to him, and I don't want to keep him from this.

"What did you say?" he asks, and I can tell he's unsure if he heard me correctly.

I smile up at him, and for the first time in the last day, it feels genuine.

"I want you to call him back, and if it's not too late, I think you should accept the job."

He shakes his head. "You don't want to move."

"I'll admit, I don't want to be that far from everyone, but I'm being completely selfish if I hold you back."

He grabs my face into his hands. "Av, I want you to be happy, too. If you're not, then there's no way in hell I will be."

I grab him tighter around the waist. "I'll be happy. I promise."

"You're positive?" He eyes me skeptically. I hope he can tell how sincere I am.

"Yes." I step back and rub the scruff on the side of his face. "Please, call him back, and let's do this."

"I fucking love you."

"I love you, too." I stand on my toes so I can kiss him, and he reciprocates. When I pull back from our kiss, I look up at him.

"What is it?"

"I hope Mallory didn't quit." I can't look him in the eye because I'm now embarrassed about my little outburst yesterday.

He grins and raises his eyebrows at me. "Why would she quit?" *Shit, he's going to think I'm psychotic.*

"I may have gone off on her for touching you yesterday."

He pulls back so he can better look at me. "Av, she's harmless, I swear."

"Well, that doesn't mean I have to like her."

He pecks me on the mouth. "Let's go get our girl and go home."

I smile at him and grab his hand.

Do I want to move? Hell no. But for this man, I'll do anything.

24

EVAN

The next week, I'm on a plane headed to Dallas with Flynn and Mallory. I had no idea that she was planning on joining us, but Flynn wanted her to get a feel for the new firm too. I can understand that, but I'm still pissed off after the shit she pulled with Avery.

After making up at her parents' house, we went home that night, put Zoey to bed, and then had hot as hell makeup sex. It almost made our fight worth it. *Almost.* Part of me feels like a dick for taking this job at all because I know that she doesn't want to leave, but I hope that I can make it up to her. She's been quiet over the last few days, and I'm pretty sure it has something to do with leaving. She doesn't seem upset with me, but her behavior has been unusual.

We had her family and Claire and Ryke over the other night to tell them all we'd be moving soon. Her parents were supportive, but it nearly crushed my sister. I feel bad leaving her after she moved out here to be with us, but I have to do this for my family. I'm just glad she has Ryke and his family now. She told me it's unfair that I'm taking another friend away from her, but then gave me a hug and told me she'd miss us.

The flight attendant announces overhead that we'll soon be landing in Dallas-Fort Worth. The purpose of this quick trip is to visit the office out here and to also hopefully find us a house. I told Avery that I'd send her pictures if I find anything promising that I think she might like. Her only request was that I find her another house with a pool.

An hour later, the three of us are finally checking into the hotel. I don't know why Flynn insisted we stay here, but I won't complain. It's fancy as shit, and I wish Avery were here with me to enjoy it.

He hands Mallory and me our keycards, and then the three of us go our separate ways, after agreeing to meet up at the hotel bar for dinner.

"Hey, did you make it?" Avery asks when I answer her call.

"Hey. Yeah, we got into Dallas about an hour ago. We just got checked into the hotel. I think I'm going to shower. I feel gross after traveling."

I hear her chuckle. "You sound like such a woman."

I throw my head back. Damn, I miss her, and I just left her this morning.

"What room are you in?"

"Five-eleven."

She pauses, most likely writing my room number down.

"What are you guys doing tonight?"

"I'm meeting Flynn and Mallory at the bar at nine.

They're supposed to have some kick-ass cheese curds." She doesn't respond. "Av, you there?"

I hear her groan. "Yeah. Why did that bitch have to go with you?"

I love her jealous side, although she has no reason to ever be jealous. Mallory can't hold a candle to my wife.

"She's not that bad." I laugh.

"She is though. She's fucking gorgeous and skinny as hell, and she knows it."

I hate when she does that. She doesn't realize how beautiful she is, and it makes me feel shitty for not reminding her more often.

"Don't do that." My voice is stern because I want her to know how serious I am.

She chuckles. "Do what?"

"Don't talk like you're not a hot ass babe." The humor is back in my voice. "Avery Porter, you are the most gorgeous woman I've ever seen." And she really is.

"Then you're either blinded by love, or you haven't seen many women in your lifetime." She has such a smart mouth. But I love it.

"I'm not blind."

I hear Zoey wailing in the background.

"She need to eat?" I ask her. I love that sweet little cry. I never thought I'd say that, but after struggling to conceive, there's no greater sound in the world.

She sighs heavily. "Yeah, call me when you get back tonight?"

I smile. "Of course. It may be late though."

"That's okay." I hear the sadness in her voice.

"You alright, Av?" I hope it's because she misses me and not because she's upset about something.

She hesitates before answering me. "Yeah, I'm just tired and hate being here without you."

Call me a selfish bastard, but that puts the smile back on my face.

"I'm glad you miss me, Mrs. Porter. Means you love me." I tease her.

"Of course, I love you, ya big loon." Zoey starts crying louder. "But I better go feed Miss Thang before she breaks my eardrums."

"She does have a set of lungs on her, just like her momma."

She gasps in mock offense. "I am not loud!"

I'm glad that she seems to be herself again.

"Okay, well, go feed our daughter. I'll call you tonight. I fucking love you."

"I fucking love you, too." I hear the smile in her voice.

By the time I take a shower and watch TV for a bit, it's time to meet Flynn and Mallory downstairs.

When I step off the elevator, I immediately see the hotel bar, On the Rocks. The restaurant is fancy as hell, and I feel underdressed in my jeans and buttoned-up polo shirt. I only brought one suit, and I plan on wearing it to meet Gerald Bowman tomorrow, so I wasn't wasting it on dinner tonight.

I take a seat at the glass-top bar, when I don't see Flynn or Mallory yet. I look around the room and notice that everything seems to be made of glass. The chandeliers that hang above the counter, have crystals that dangle low, and each has a different colored bulb. The place has an interesting vibe. Being an interior designer, Avery would love it.

I feel like there's been a huge wedge between us, but

I'm going to try like hell to make it better. Maybe this move is exactly what we both need.

"There you are." I look up at the sound of Mallory's voice.

"Hey, Mallory. Have you seen Flynn?"

She takes the stool beside me. "No, he sent us a group text and said he had to go into the office to meet up with Gerald. I have no idea what for this time of night."

Just my luck. Avery will be pissed when she finds out that I met with Mallory by myself. I know she trusts me, but she doesn't trust her.

I pull my phone out of my pocket, and sure enough, I have a missed text from him.

"I didn't see it." I stick my phone back in my pocket. "Well, you wanna eat? I kind of want to call it an early night anyway after traveling." I can't be a dick, so I guess I'm stuck here with her. I'll eat and then go back to my room and call my wife.

"Actually," she bats her fake lashes at me, "I was thinking we could go up to my room and order room service."

Jesus Christ. This woman has no filter.

"Um …" I dig in my pocket for my wallet and lay a twenty on the counter. "I'm actually going to call it an early night."

I go to stand, but she grabs my arm.

"Come on, Evan. I could show you a real good time."

I yank my arm from her grasp. "I have to leave." I grit out and then turn on my heels as fast as I can. I need to get away from her.

25

EVAN

When I make it back to my room, I take my phone out of my jeans before throwing myself down on the bed. I pull up Avery's name, but my mind keeps racing after the stint Mallory just pulled. *What the hell is she up to?* There's a knock at the door. I'm guessing it's Flynn.

I don't bother looking through the hole in the door, which is a big mistake.

"Is everything okay?" I ask, only because I have to be nice to her because she's my boss's niece.

She hiccups a cry.

"Can-can I come in?" I throw my head back in frustration. I'm sure I look like a dick, but nothing about this makes me comfortable. When I don't answer her, she goes on. "Please?" She cries loudly, and I'm worried that someone is going to come out to the hallway because she's disturbing them.

She doesn't let me respond, but instead pushes past me, into my room.

"Mallory, this looks really inappropriate. I don't mean to be an ass, but you really shouldn't be here."

She plops down on my bed, and I'm about to pull my damn hair out.

"He-he broke up with me." Oh Jesus. Why couldn't she have called a girlfriend about this? Why did she come running to me? And why the hell was she propositioning me downstairs when she had a boyfriend?

I sit on the couch across from the bed.

"Your boyfriend broke up with you?" Maybe if I give in, she'll leave sooner.

She nods frantically as she continues to cry. Maybe I'm heartless, but I really don't want to deal with her tonight. I'm supposed to be on the phone with Avery right now.

"Yes. I called him on the way up to my room, and he told me that he doesn't want a long-distance relationship. I wanted to marry him, but I need this job."

I sigh before standing up and taking the seat next to her on the bed. As soon as I do, I regret it, but I pat her on the back. I feel like an idiot, because she takes that as an invitation to move closer to me, and then she lays her damn head on my shoulder. I'm now patting her shoulder awkwardly.

I try to stand from the bed, but she latches on to me like a damn leech.

"Please, don't go," she looks up at me, and then the next thing I know, she's leaning into me.

I fly off the bed like my ass is on fire.

"You should probably go back to your room. We have an early morning," I say sternly.

"Please don't make me stay by myself," she says in an extremely seductive voice, that makes the hairs on the back of my neck stand at attention. I fucking hate the position she's put me in. Flynn will be finding out about this, and I don't give a damn if it puts me at risk of losing my job.

I shake my head. "Mallory, please leave. I need to call my wife."

"But Evan." She sobs, and honestly, I couldn't care less. "What does that bitch have that I don't?" *Oh. My. Fucking. God.* What the hell have I gotten myself into?

"Out!" I roar, and I'd be surprised if the people in the next room over didn't just hear my outburst.

She stands from the bed and then pulls her shirt off and is now standing in front of me in only her bra and skirt. *Fuck my life.*

I turn on my heels and slam the door behind me.

I can't hear myself think over the ringing in my ears. I didn't even do anything wrong, but I know that Avery would be pissed if she knew what just happened. Not that I plan on keeping it a secret from her, but who the hell wants to tell their wife that a woman she envies was just half naked in his hotel room? Not me. That's for sure.

I push the buttons on the elevator, willing it to open so I can get the fuck away from her. Once it finally arrives, I press the button to the main floor. Looks like I'll be getting another room.

"Can I help you, sir?" The blonde behind the front desk asks. I just hope that I can find another room this late.

"Yeah, I need a room."

She eyes me skeptically, probably confused as to why I don't have any luggage with me.

"Uh, yeah sure." She looks at her computer screen.

"You're in luck because I have one more room on the tenth floor."

I slam my hand on the counter. "Perfect, I'll take it."

I give her my ID and credit card, and then after she hands me my new keycard, I make my way to the tenth floor.

When I get to my room, I go to the bathroom and then use some of the complementary mouthwash. I need to call Avery still.

I reach into my pocket and then realize that I left my phone in my other room. *Fuck.*

I pick up the hotel phone and quickly dial her, desperately wanting to hear my wife's voice. I decide against telling her about Mallory's stunt tonight. I don't think that's something I should tell her over the phone.

The call goes straight to voicemail, which is strange because her phone is never off. She must have let her battery die.

I click the TV on and watch a mindless reality show and then decide to try Avery one more time before I go to bed. I'm so damn tired but want to talk to her before I go to sleep.

I dial her, but then once again, get no response. I'm starting to worry that something is wrong with her or Zoey.

26

AVERY

I still haven't heard from Evan, but I'm not surprised after he told me it would probably be late. When I put Zoey to bed, I sat on the couch and watched reruns of *Friends* on Netflix, and then when I got bored with that, I finished the smutty romance book I'd been reading for the last few days. I hate being in this big house by myself, but I'm glad that he'll only be gone for a couple nights.

I'm guessing the three of them are still at the bar having drinks, so I decide to take a bubble bath. As soon as I strip out of my clothes, I feel the water with my foot and then sink down into the massive claw tub. Evan had this put in for me when we moved here. I don't know why, but I'd always wanted one, so he made it happen. But this isn't your average claw tub. No, this one is big enough to comfortably fit four people. Of course, it's only ever been used for me and him, but it's heavenly. I never thought I'd be a fan of bathtub sex, but this thing makes it doable.

As soon as my ass hits the bottom of the tub, I relax into the lavender scented bubbles. I can feel the stress of the last few weeks wash away. Maybe I gave into Evan too easily last week when I agreed to go to Dallas, because frankly, I don't want to leave, but I want him to be happy. I want us both to be happy, and maybe this is the answer. I just want to be wherever our marriage is going to be alright. Our relationship has continued to stay strong throughout the years. We endured infertility, for Christ's sake. Surely, we can get through a cross-country move.

My husband and daughter are the two most important people in my life, and as long as I have them, I'm convinced that everything will be just fine.

I rinse the bubbles from my naked form and then wrap myself in a towel. I'd do just about anything for a glass of wine right now, but since I'm still nursing, I head to the kitchen for a Dr. Pepper. Not as wonderful as alcohol, but probably better since I have to be coherent for Zo in the morning.

Once I'm dressed and lying in bed, I grab my phone off the end table, but then realize it's dead, so I plug it in.

I don't know if he tried calling while I was in the tub, but if he did, he's probably worried. His overprotectiveness drives me bat shit sometimes, but I love him for it.

After getting up to feed Zoey and then changing her before putting her back to bed, I check my phone, and it's fully charged. I'm guessing he's just now getting back to his room, so I dial him.

"Hello?" *A woman.* Is that fucking Mallory? Why is Mallory answering his phone? They must still be at the bar. He probably left his phone to go to the bathroom or to get another drink. But it's awfully quiet for them being in a noisy restaurant.

"Mallory?"

She doesn't respond right away, and I hear movement in the background.

"Avery? Oh, hey. Did you need something?" she asks in a drowsy voice. Was she fucking sleeping? Why does she have his phone?

Has this bitch lost her mind? She's answering my husband's phone, and she's asking me if I need something.

"Where's Evan?"

"I think he's in the shower."

What. The. Fuck?

"Why the fuck are you in my husband's hotel room? Let me talk to him. Now!" Maybe I'm being irrational, but I lost all rationality as soon as she answered my husband's phone.

"Sweetheart, I hate to be the one to tell you this, but he doesn't want you. He took this job because he knew you didn't want to come to Dallas with him."

"Put him on the phone." I seethe.

"I told you he's in the shower." She pauses. "Oh, my God! That man has a magical tongue. If I would have known that, I would have fucked him a lot sooner." She chuckles.

"You're a lying bitch." I can barely contain my rage at this point. I know I shouldn't give into her, but I want to know what the hell is going on.

I hang up the phone and then quickly Google the phone number to the hotel. Evan gave me his room number when he got in earlier.

The phone rings twice before it's answered.

"Hello?"

My world spins. I can't see straight, and I think I'm about to throw up. Did he sleep with her? What the fuck? No, he wouldn't do that to me. Would he?

"Hello?" Mallory says again.

"Where is my husband?" I growl into the phone and then hear a door open in the background.

"There you are." She coos.

"Who are you talking to?" I hear Evan, and now I have my answer.

I drop my phone on the floor without ending the call and sprint to the bathroom. Everything I ate comes up once I'm hovering over the toilet. I know that there's been a lot of tension between us lately, but I didn't realize it was so bad that he would run to someone else. Another woman.

This explains why he always blew me off when I got pissed about her advances. He was fucking her and tried to make it seem like no big deal. I've been such an idiot.

Once I'm done throwing up, I hug the seat, and my tears drip into the bowl. I can't believe this is happening. I can't believe he just threw away the last ten years of our lives. How could he do this to me? To our daughter?

It hurts. It hurts so bad. The pain in my chest is the worst I've ever experienced.

I pull myself from the toilet and lean my back up against the wall. Immediately, my breathing becomes rapid, and I feel like I might be having a heart attack. This must be a panic attack. I hate that I'm by myself while I'm feeling this way, since Zoey is in the other room.

Once I'm finally feeling better, I lay on the bathroom floor, my face pressed against the cold tile.

My head is pounding, and I'm still feeling sick to my stomach at the thought of my husband with that bitch, but I drift in and out of sleep until Zoey's cries stir me awake.

❦ 27 ❦

EVAN

The next morning, I wake from a restless sleep. I ended up going back to my other room last night to get my phone because I was getting worried about Avery. It's unlike her to keep her phone dead that long. Mallory was on the hotel phone when I walked in, and she was once again acting like a flirtatious bitch, but I quickly grabbed my phone and left.

When I got back to this room, I tried calling her again, even though it was late, but still got no answer.

I look at the clock next to the bed, and it's seven in the morning, which means it's even earlier back home. I reach for my phone, knowing that she's most likely up with the baby now, so I should be able to reach her.

She finally picks up.

"How could you?" She seethes, and I have no fucking clue what she's talking about. I can tell by the crack in her voice, that she's been crying. *What the hell happened?*

"Baby, what's wrong?"

"Don't 'baby' me, Evan! I'm fucking done."

I take a deep breath, trying to calm myself because I'm trying to understand what the hell she thinks I did.

"Avery, I have no damn clue what you're talking about, but I've been trying to get a hold of you since last night. Why didn't you answer your phone?"

"No!" she screams and nearly blasts my eardrum. "You don't get to put this on me! Tomorrow, when you get home, we won't be here."

She's leaving me? I don't even know what in God's name I did.

"What?" I know she can hear the emotion in my voice. "Av, if this is about moving, I'll turn the damn job down." I stand from the bed and pull my laptop out of its bag. "I'm booking a flight now. Please, don't go."

"You know this isn't about fucking Dallas." I hear her disconnect the line, and I'm left wondering how the hell things got like this.

I try calling her back, but I'm sent to her voicemail.

"Hey, this is Avery…."

I hit 'end' and then launch my phone into the TV across the room and immediately crack the screen and most likely broke my phone too. *Shit.* Looks like I'll be buying a new TV for the damn hotel.

I pull at my hair and scream.

"Fuuuuck!"

I know things have been tense between us lately, but I thought we were okay yesterday when I left.

I pick my phone up off the ground and pull my sister's number up.

"Evan, you better be dying if you're calling me this early," she says when she answers. I forgot how early it is, but I don't care right now.

"Claire, I need you to go check on Avery." I rush out.

"What the hell are you talking about? Is she okay?" I hear rustling in the background.

"No." I croak out. "I don't know. Something is going on, and she won't tell me what, but she said that when I get home tomorrow, she and Zoey won't be there."

"What?" she whisper yells. "Why the fuck would she leave you?"

"Your guess is as good as mine." I slide down the wall. "I'm booking a flight home now, but please go over there."

"Yeah. Yeah, okay." She sighs. "Ev, I don't know what's going on between you two right now, but you need to make it right."

"I know, but how can I make it right if I have no damn clue what the hell she's mad at me for?"

"I don't know, but you better figure it out."

After reassuring me that she'll check on Avery, we hang up. I quickly book my flight and then send a quick text to Flynn, letting him know that something urgent came up and that I have to leave right away.

"Hello?" I answer my phone on the first ring.

"Evan, is everything okay?" Flynn asks from the other line.

"Yeah." I clear my throat, not wanting him to hear how upset I am. "I just need to get home."

"Okay." He pauses. "Get packed up, and I'll get you an Uber to the airport."

"Thank you, sir."

"You're welcome. Oh, and Evan?"

"Yeah, Flynn?" I ask as I rush to pack up the few things I have with me.

"What do you want me to tell Gerald this morning?"

I grunt into the phone. "Tell him I'm no longer interested."

That's the only answer I can give them right now. I have no clue what is happening to my marriage, but I know that I can't up and move to Dallas.

"I understand," he says in a disappointed voice. "Good luck with everything, and I'll see you Monday."

❧ 28 ❧

AVERY

Thank God my mom came to get Zoey this morning because I was hardly able to pull myself out of bed.

I'm wrapped in several blankets, when I hear a pounding on the front door. I have a feeling it's Claire because knowing Evan, he sent her to check on me. I checked the flight schedule online, and his flight lands in three hours. That gives me three hours to figure out where I'm going to go. Three hours to decide where I'm going to uproot our newborn daughter. I could just tell him not to come home, but I can't stay here. I can't stay within these walls where all our memories lay. Right now, it's almost unbearable to be in the bed we've shared. A part of me has to wonder if he ever brought someone back to our home. The home we've shared. The home we worked hard to buy together. The home we suffered through infertility in. The home where we brought our newborn daughter from the hospital. How long has this been going on? How many other women has my husband been screwing behind my back? The thought makes me want to vomit again, but instead, I pull my ass out of bed to answer the door. By now, the knocking is becoming more frantic.

I pull the front door open, and sure enough, Claire is standing on the front porch.

"My God, Av. Are you alright?"

I groan. "What do you want, Claire?"

She pushes past me, without being invited inside. I'm really not in the mood for this.

"Why don't you tell me what is going on?" She raises her eyebrows at me while her hands rest on her hips. "My brother called me freaking out because you told him you're leaving him, and he has no idea why."

I give a manic laugh, and I know I sound like a damn psycho.

"He's a fucking liar if he says he doesn't know."

"Well, I don't know what's going on, so why don't you fill me in?"

I throw myself on the couch, trying to make myself comfortable because I know that she's not going to leave until I talk to her.

She plops down in one of our recliners and stares at me. She obviously thinks this is my fault.

"He slept with Mallory," I say pointedly.

She gasps and shakes her head. "No. No way. He'd never do that to you."

She stands from the chair and starts pacing the length of the living room, and she's making me a nervous wreck.

"Would you sit the hell down?"

She stops in her tracks and then pulls at her hair as she lands herself in the chair again.

"Why the hell do you think he cheated on you? And with Mallory nonetheless?"

"Claire, I'm not just making accusations. I'm not that much of a bitch." I give her a heated stare. Of course, she would take her brother's side in all of this. I guess I can't really say I blame her, considering he is the only family she has.

She sighs. "You're right. I'm sorry." She lays her head on the back of the chair. "What happened?"

"I called his phone last night, and she answered."

"Are you sure he slept with her?" She cringes. Obviously uncomfortable discussing her brother like this.

I wipe at the tear that runs down my face, but it's pointless because others follow close behind.

I sniff. "At first, I didn't believe her, but when I hung up on her and called his hotel room, she answered again, and then I heard him talking in the background."

She gasps, and her jaw nearly hits the floor.

"I'm going to kill him."

I shake my head. "Things have been shit between us lately, but I didn't know it had gone this far."

She stands, and then in the next instant, I'm in her arms. I don't know how long I cry, but when I finally lift my head from her shoulder, I'm convinced that I'm dehydrated from all the tears that have fallen over the last several hours.

I pull myself away from her. I feel bad that she's been put between us, but I'm glad she's here.

"I need to talk to my parents about staying with them for a bit."

She shakes her head. "No, Evan can stay with us." I really don't want to stay here with all the memories, but it would probably be best for Zoey. I may have to move us somewhere else eventually though.

I sigh. It breaks my heart. I'm not just losing my husband, I'm losing my best friend too.

She rubs at my hair.

"I don't know what the hell is up with my brother, but you're still my sister, okay?"

I look up at her and nod.

"It hurts so bad. How did you get through it?"

"I had you and Evan, and then I found Ryke," she says sympathetically.

I rest my head on her shoulder and eventually drift back to sleep.

I STIR awake at the sound of the garage door opening. I look around, realizing Claire must have left sometime after I fell asleep. My stomach drops at the thought of having to confront Evan, again. It was bad enough talking to him on the phone this morning, but now I have to face him. I have to decide what I'm going to do next. If he wants to stay in the house, there's no way in hell I'll be staying here too. What he did is unforgivable.

As soon as I hear the door close behind him, I sit up on the couch. I wipe the drool from my face and rub at my eyes that are surely bloodshot as a result of crying for hours. To top it off, my head feels like a damn train ran into it.

When I see him standing in the doorway, my breath hitches, and my heart breaks all over again. I want to scream at him, maybe even hit him right now, but I can't find the energy for either of those things. I feel like I've been put through the wringer. I think I could sleep for a week. Unfortunately, I can't do that.

"Av," he whispers, and my walls crumble.

The tears I thought had dried up, flow freely down my face. I've never cried so much in my life. I've also never had my heart obliterated either. I gave this man my heart, and he destroyed it. I know that there's no way we can ever come back from this.

I try standing from the couch, but lose my balance. I realize that I feel like shit after not eating all day and throwing up everything I ate yesterday.

He crosses the room and grabs my arms to try to steady me, but I flinch at his touch. It's as if he's burnt me. Which is funny, because metaphorically speaking, he did.

"Don't." I seethe. I find my balance and then push past him.

"Avery, we have to talk about this," he says to my back as I'm walking toward our bedroom. I stink and probably need to take a shower, but right now, I just want to crawl back under the covers and sleep the rest of the day away.

I turn back to him, and I'm sure the look on my face is terrifying.

"I don't want to talk to you, Evan. There's nothing to fucking talk about!" I shout and then realize I'm shaking.

He starts toward me, but then stops himself.

"Av, you're shaking. Please come sit down."

"No. I need to get a shower and then get Zoey from my mom's." I pause. "Do I need to go stay with them or are you leaving?"

He chuckles and then throws his head back in frustration.

"You have got to be fucking kidding me. I have no damn clue what the hell I did. Don't you think you at least owe me that?"

"I don't owe you a goddamned thing. Claire said you can stay with her."

I turn to walk away and then hear a crash behind me. I jump. When I turn to see what the sound was, a lamp we got as a wedding gift, is broken to pieces up against the wall.

"I can't do this anymore," I choke out.

Without another word, I head to our room and close the door behind me. I slide down to the floor, and once again, I break.

❦ 29 ❦

EVAN

I've been driving around for the last forty-five minutes and have no fucking clue where I'm at. I haven't been paying attention to what's going on around me, so it's a damn miracle I haven't gotten myself killed yet.

I can't do this anymore.

Her words keep replaying in my head. How did things get this bad? I love that woman with every fiber of my being, but apparently, that isn't enough.

I finally pull into Claire and Ryke's driveway and debate whether or not I should even bother knocking on the door. I don't feel like talking about this anymore, but maybe Claire knows what the hell is going on.

Sighing in frustration, I get out of the Jeep.

"How could you do that to her?" Claire screams as soon as she opens the front door. In the next instant, she's pulling me into the house and then pounding her fists into my chest. For being so much smaller than me, she sure is tough as hell.

I grab her hands to stop her.

"Will you please tell me what the fuck is going on? Everyone seems to know, but me."

She finally stops hitting me and backs up but is breathing heavy. I wouldn't be surprised if she started attacking again.

"After all the shit I went through with Trevor and how much pain you saw that caused me, how could you sleep with that bitch?"

What. The. Actual. Fuck? I become dizzy, so I have to grab the wall behind me. *She thinks I cheated on her?*

"She-she thinks I cheated on her?" I choke out.

"How could you?" she screams, ignoring my question. "You just had a child with her, for Christ's sake!"

I pull at my hair.

"I didn't fucking cheat on her! Why the hell would she even think that?"

She turns and heads for the living room, and I follow. Once we enter the room, she throws herself down on the couch.

"Gee, I don't know. Maybe because fucking Mallory answered your phone the other night *and* she heard you talking."

My mind races, trying to connect all the dots. What the fuck is she talking about? *Oh, shit.*

"Fuck!" I yell.

"Ev?" she asks hesitatingly.

I look up at her, and I'm sure I look like I've been backed over with a truck.

"Did you cheat on her?"

"What?" I shake my head. "Do you honestly believe I'd do that to her?"

She runs her hands through her hair.

"I don't know what to believe, but I do know that she is crushed." She stands. "I need to go check on Aria."

This has possibly been the worst day of my life. How did my marriage come to this? A year ago, she would have never thought for one minute that I was capable of doing something so terrible to her. Have we grown apart that much, that she can't even trust me anymore?

I'd never dream of doing something like that. Ever. In a million years. I don't care how shitty our marriage gets, I'd never resort to cheating on my wife. I just wish she understood how much I love her.

"Eben!" I look up at the sound of my nephew's voice, and I force a smile on my face.

"Hey, bud." I reach my hand out to him to do knuckles. Something we've been doing since he was old enough to know how.

"Where's Avvy?" he asks as he climbs onto my lap. "And Zo?"

I pat his head. "They're at home. You'll see them soon, okay?" I hope that I'm not lying.

Not only am I losing my wife, I'm losing my baby girl. I don't know if I can go on without them. Those two are the reason I get up every morning. Now, I feel like my life has come to a complete stop.

"Okay!" He jumps from my lap and then is sprinting down the hallway, like the ball of energy he is. I'm jealous of how innocent that kid is.

Claire walks back into the room with Aria in her arms.

"Is Ryke working?" I ask as I stand to walk to the kitchen to get a drink.

"Yeah," she says behind me. "But don't even think

about going over there. The last thing I need is to take care of your drunk ass because you're depressed."

"Whatever, sis," I mumble as I open the fridge. I take a gulp of water, and then I turn back to her. "I need a place to stay."

She puts Aria in her high chair.

"I know you do, but I'm pissed at you."

I throw my hands in the air. "Jesus Christ, sis. I didn't cheat on her!"

"Then why the hell was Mallory in your hotel room?" She raises her eyebrows at me.

I lean on the counter. "She came to my room crying because apparently her boyfriend broke up with her last night. I didn't think I should be an ass considering she's my boss' niece, but then she kind of took off her shirt and basically threw herself at me."

Her hand flies to her mouth as she gasps.

"Evan!" Okay, that probably didn't help my case about not cheating.

"Claire, I didn't fucking ask her to come to my room, and I sure as hell didn't want her taking her clothes off. *God.* She's a bitch." I sigh, as I pull at my hair in defeat. "I left and got another room."

"Well, even if I did believe you, I'm not saying I do, but if I did, that doesn't mean that Avery does."

"You know what? This is bullshit. I'll go stay in a fucking hotel."

I storm out of the room, toward the front door.

"Yeah, you do that. Maybe Mallory will join you later."

I love my sister, but she sure knows how to piss me off, and right now, she's doing a good job of that.

"I thought you knew me better," I say with my back to

her and my hand on the doorknob. I have no clue where the hell I'm going to go.

"So did I."

Great. Now my wife and my sister are both pissed at me. Can this day get any more shitty?

30

AVERY

Evan left two weeks ago. I thought the pain would lessen a bit, but it seems to have only gotten worse as time has gone by. He has tried calling and texting me, but I can't bring myself to talk to him yet. He hasn't come by the house again, which I'm honestly surprised by, but at the same time, I'm glad.

He's been taking Zoey for a couple hours throughout the week after he gets off work. He got the firm to let him work earlier in the morning, and then he leaves work before I'm off and gets her from my mom's. I've done everything I could to avoid running into him.

I've talked to Claire a few times, but she hasn't said much about him. She's only called to check in. I have a feeling she's worried about upsetting me.

"Hi pretty girl!" I clap my hands at Zoey and then sit on the floor next to her. My mom has her propped up against her nursing pillow. I can't believe that soon she'll be sitting on her own. Where has the time gone?

I grab her toy monkey and squeeze it to make it

squeak. The damn thing is annoying, but it makes her laugh. The sound of her giggles makes my heart feel a little less heavy.

I look up and see my mom's sympathetic look.

"Hi, Mom," I lift Zo from the floor. "Did she have a good day?"

"Yeah. She just ate about an hour ago and had her diaper changed. She really liked the carrots you sent."

I tweak Zoey's nose.

"We have to be careful not to feed her too much of it because Claire said Aria's nose turned orange from all the carrots she ate." I laugh. "We don't need that, do we Zo?" I kiss her forehead, and she swats at my face.

Mom laughs. "No, I guess we don't. Tomorrow, we'll try the green beans."

I gather her things and then leave so we can get home at a decent time. Since Evan left, I've preferred to be locked inside the house before it gets dark out. Not that we live in a rough area, but he made me feel safe. *Fuck.* I really shouldn't think about him. I miss him so damn much, but I need to stay busy to keep my mind off of him. Luckily, during the week, I stay busy at the office and with Zo, but it's when I'm by myself at night. For the last two weeks, I've dreamt of him and finding out about Mallory. Almost every day since he left, I've had to relive the hell he put me through. I've woken up crying, but I have no one by my side to help ease the pain.

Once we're home, I put Zoey in her swing and then fix a bowl of cereal. It's pointless to make a big dinner for only me. When I walk back to the living room, she's batting at her toys dangling from the mobile above her head.

"What should we watch tonight, Zo?" I flip the TV on and quickly get lost in a rerun of *Friends*. This is by far the best show ever made. I had actually wanted to name Zoey, Phoebe instead, but Evan wasn't having it. I guess it wouldn't have been nice of me to name my child after the quirky character, but she was always my favorite.

I look over at Zo, and she's now sound asleep.

"Well, you aren't any fun," I murmur.

Apparently, I've resorted to talking to myself now. Am I that lonely? I've always thought I was independent, but that doesn't mean I don't miss the companionship. Actually, I can be honest. I miss Evan so damn much, but I know that things are never going to be the same. I think I'm a pretty forgiving person, but I draw the line at cheating. I'd never in a million years dream of hurting him the way he did me.

I decide to leave my sleeping babe alone for now and pick my phone up to see if I have any missed calls or texts. I'm the worst about turning my ringer on after work. Charlotte has a big no cell phone policy, so I'm always careful. As much as I can't stand the woman, I do need my job.

I see that I have a text from Sierra. I feel like I've been the worst friend since she moved to North Carolina. I'm surprised she still wants to talk to me. She lost her husband, and I'm over here sulking like the bitch I am.

Deciding I really need to talk to her, I forego texting and call her instead.

"Hey, stranger." She answers after the first ring.

"Hey. How's everything going in the Carolina's?" I've never been to the East Coast, but the pictures she sent me looked amazing.

"Okay. Just been helping Grandma Rose at the bakery and keeping busy with the boys."

"How's Augs and little Jayce?" I hate that they live so far now because all of our kids would have been the best of friends.

"They are good. Growing too damn fast."

I can hear the sadness in her voice, which makes me feel even worse about not keeping in touch with her.

"Sier, I'm so sorry I haven't called much since Zo was born."

"Girl, you've been busy." She pauses. "How are things with you and Evan?" I can hear the hesitation in her voice. I should have known that Claire would tell her about our split.

I sigh. "Not good. Sier, he hurt me so damn bad." I really don't want to spend the night talking about my shitty marriage.

"You think you can get a week off from work?"

I perk up at the idea.

"I don't know. Maybe." I'm not sure they'd appreciate me leaving again after just being on leave for so long.

"Why don't you and Zo come out here? Escape for a bit. Could be good for you to clear your mind. The salty sea air is good at making anyone feel better."

I smile. "That actually sounds heavenly. You sure your grandma won't mind if we crash with you guys?"

I can hear the smile in her voice. "No. She'll love it, and I know she'll love Zo too."

"Okay. Let me talk to Charlotte, and then I'll get back to you."

"Sounds good. I think we could both use some bestie

time. I've gotta go. I hear Jayce crying, but text me once you know when you can come out."

"Sounds good. Love you, Momma." I make a kissing sound into the phone, and she chuckles before we both hang up.

After getting Zoey settled in her bed, I collapse into mine. I'm in desperate need of a sleeping pill, but know I wouldn't be able to get up with her in the middle of the night. I turn toward the empty side of the bed, and I grab his pillow and hope and pray that I'll be able to sleep. I close my eyes but am immediately wide awake again when I hear a knocking noise outside. When it stops, I close my eyes again, but then it gets louder. I'm sure it's only the wind, but I'm half tempted to get my baby from the other room. I know I'm being silly, but before, Evan would always check to make sure everything was alright. Now, there's only me to do that.

Realizing that I'm overreacting, I grab my phone off the end table and tuck it under my pillow.

I finally fall asleep and, once again, dream of Evan.

31

EVAN

"Hey, man," Malcom says as he takes the seat across from me at Ryke's. He insisted that we go out tonight, to celebrate our buy-out of the firm. It took a lot of convincing on our part, but Flynn finally agreed that we would make a good team. I honestly think we can make the place a hell of a lot better. Plus, I knew that I couldn't go to Dallas. Even if my marriage takes the piss, I can't leave my daughter.

"Hey." I sip at the Corona Ryke brought me. He's off soon and said he'd join us.

After my sister nearly killed me a couple weeks ago, he called and told me to get my ass back to their house. I can tell Claire is still pissed off at me and not sure what to believe, but at least I have a place to stay. It sucks, but I can't really blame her after what her deadbeat ex-husband did to her. But I'm nothing like Trevor Davis. I'd give anything to be back home with my wife and daughter, but I can't see that happening anytime soon. The fact that she thinks I'm capable of hurting her like that, guts me.

Malcom grabs the menu in front of him. "What's good here? I haven't been here since it was just the bar," he asks, bringing me back to the present.

"The mushroom burger is fucking amazing, or Avery likes the turkey club." Shit. I know he's going to lecture me for mentioning her.

He raises his eyebrows at me. "Damn, dude. You've got it bad. What has this woman done to you?"

I sigh and throw my head back against the booth. "I fucking miss her, but she refuses to talk to me, much less see me when I drop by to get Zoey." I sigh. "I'll never get her to believe me if she doesn't listen."

I chug the rest of my beer and then slam the bottle on the table.

"Dude, you need to show her who's the boss."

I chuckle at him. "What do you know about relationships?" Now I'm the one to raise my eyebrows at him.

He balls his napkin up and throws it at my head, and I guffaw.

"Fuck you." He laughs. "Okay, you got me there. I don't know a damn thing about relationships, much less being married, but I do know that if you want something bad enough you shouldn't just give up trying, because it might not always be there."

I'll admit, I'm stunned into silence.

"Shit. That's deep." I see a look on his face that I don't recognize, and I have to wonder if he's speaking from experience.

"Don't get used to it, asshole." He looks at me over his drink. "I may not be marriage material, but you are, man, and I know that woman loves you. Maybe she just needs you to remind her how good you two are together."

"Alright Mr. Love Doctor. How do you suppose I do that? Remember, she thinks I'm a cheating asshole."

"Well, she's got the asshole part right." He winks at me like an idiot.

"Fucker," I mumble.

"Ask her out on a date." He states matter-of-factly. *Say what?*

"You think I should ask my wife out on a date? The woman who won't even talk to me. She wants nothing to do with me. She has done everything she can to avoid me like the fucking plague."

He shrugs. "I don't think it'll hurt anything. Start over with her. Show her what made her fall in love with you all those years ago."

I contemplate his words and then laugh. "Yeah, okay. Well, I'm pretty sure me fucking another woman isn't what made her fall in love with me."

"Did you fuck Mallory?"

"What the hell, asshole? No, I didn't fuck anyone besides my wife." I can feel my hackles rising, and I'm sure my face is beet red with anger.

"Well, then, you shouldn't have anything to worry about."

I huff. "You make it sound so easy. She can't fucking trust me. In her mind, I did the worst imaginable thing a man could do to his wife."

"Well, try it. Maybe she'll hear you out if you woo her with flowers and wine."

I shake my head at him, but inside I'm contemplating it. I'll never get my wife back if I don't get a chance to explain to her that what she thinks is wrong.

"Who wants cheese fries?" Ryke hollers as he places the

cheese-covered potatoes in front of us. Damn, they smell good.

"Ryke, you remember my buddy Malcom?"

"Yeah, man. Good to see you." He reaches his hand across the table to shake Malcom's.

"You too," he says around a bite of fries. "I like what you've done with the place." He waves his arm in the air.

Ryke nods. "Thanks. I've got a family now, so I wanted to make it a little friendlier for the kids, you know?"

Malcom doesn't know, but he nods his head. "I like it."

We visit for the next hour, and I'll admit, it feels good to not sit around feeling sorry for myself.

I tell the guys bye and head out to the parking lot.

After coming back from Dallas, I had a nice long chat with Flynn about his bitch niece. He, of course, questioned me about sleeping with her, which was uncomfortable as shit, but finally realized that I was telling the truth. Thank fuck he fired her. I honestly didn't think he would. That's at least one less thing I have to worry about every day. I'd never have a chance at getting my wife back if she was there to screw things up even more.

My phone chimes in my pocket, and I see Lucy is calling.

"Hey, Luc. Everything okay?"

"Hey, Evan. Yeah, everything's fine, but Avery just called me saying she threw up at work today, so I told her to go home and I'd keep Zoey. You want to come see her?"

Fuck. My girl is sick and no one is home to take care of her. She's stubborn as hell, but I don't care anymore. I'm done being ignored.

I run my hands through my hair. "Yeah, of course."

I head toward Lucy and Ed's house, trying to come up

with a plan. Malcom's words run through my head. *Show her who's boss.* I don't want to be an asshole because that'll push her even further away, so I've got to think of a well-thought-out plan. My girl is not going to be easy on me. I think the thing that hurts the most is that, if the situation were reversed, I wouldn't for one second think she was capable of hurting me so deep.

"THERE'S DADDY'S GIRL." I lift my daughter into my arms and kiss her cheek. I hate being away from her so much. Avery has thankfully not fought me on seeing her, but it's not the same. I want both my girls back. I just don't know how to get that yet.

My little dark-haired beauty giggles at me as I blow raspberries on her belly. I'm glad she's young and won't remember any of this, but I just hope that one day soon we'll all be back together as a family.

I look up and see my mother-in-law's concerned expression.

"You doing okay?" The last thing I need is anyone feeling sorry for me.

I take a deep breath and then release it. "Yeah. I just miss them." I don't have it in me to lie because I do miss them like crazy. At least I get to see one of them tonight.

"She'll come around. I don't know what happened between the two of you, but don't give up on her." If she knew why Avery kicked me out, she probably wouldn't be so sympathetic.

"Thanks Luc." I give her a side hug and then walk into the living room with Zoey.

"Why don't you stay for dinner? I've got a roast in the oven that'll be done soon."

I nod at her and then look down at my daughter. "Sounds good. Thanks." I'm not sure how Avery would feel if she knew I was eating dinner with her family, but if it allows me to spend more time with my daughter, I'll deal with the consequences later.

Lucy turns back to the kitchen, so I grab some of Zo's toys and place them around us on the floor. I know that I see her a lot, but I still worry that I'm going to miss out on something important.

"Daddy will be home soon, baby girl." I kiss her forehead and hope like hell that my words ring true.

❦ 32 ❧

AVERY

I'm pretty sure I'm dying. I don't think I've ever been this sick in my life. I'm beginning to get well acquainted with the porcelain throne. I didn't know it was possible to throw up this much. Totally disgusting, and I'm ready to go to bed. Thank God my parents offered to keep Zoey tonight because there's no way in hell I could take care of her.

"Hey, babe." I didn't hear Carly come back. She drove me home earlier, and I left my car at work because she was worried I wouldn't make it home without getting sick. "Feeling any better?" I hear the water turn on, and then she's handing me a wet washcloth.

"No. I'm going to die." I moan.

She chuckles. "I won't let you die. Come on, why don't you try to drink some Sprite?"

I have no desire to try to stand from the floor, but I know I need something in my stomach. She lifts me up, and I'm hit with a wave of nausea again.

I slam the toilet lid shut and then sit and lay my head on the counter.

"I'll just sleep here tonight." I turn my head when I see a plastic bag sitting on the counter out of the corner of my eye.

"What's in the bag?" I hope she's not going to try to get me to eat. I can't eat.

When I look up at her, I can tell she's worried that I'm not going to like what she's about to say.

"Spill it," I mumble.

"Av, you've been puking all day. Nobody else at work is sick. There's only one explanation." Then it hits me. *She thinks I'm fucking pregnant.* There's no way. Well, there is a way, but how could I get pregnant so soon after struggling so long to have Zoey?

"You think I'm pregnant?" Suddenly, the urge to throw up is at the back of my mind.

"I don't know, but I think we need to find out."

She opens the box and gets the stick of truth out. This is going to be the longest three fucking minutes of my life.

"This one is supposed to be super good. It'll say positive or negative so you don't have to worry if the lines don't show up clearly." She sets it on the counter next to me. "I'll give you some privacy, but pee on the stick, and I'll be back in a few."

I almost wish she'd stay while I do this. I may need her to hold me up if I pass out in shock. This is the kind of bad luck I've been having lately, so it shouldn't even surprise me. How am I going to take care of two babies by myself?

I do as Carly said and pee on the stick and then set a

timer on my phone. If I stare at the clock while I wait, it'll seem like forever.

I scroll through Facebook and then Instagram and don't see anything exciting posted. I jump at the sound of the alarm going off.

Here goes nothing.

Negative.

I release the breath I didn't realize I was holding. I love being a mother, but I can't imagine trying to juggle a full-time job and taking care of two children all on my own. I know that Evan would help, like he does with Zoey, but it would be hard.

Carly knocks on the door and then opens it before I respond.

"What'd it say?"

I hold the stick up. "Negative." I glare up at her. "Thanks for freaking the fuck out of me."

She laughs. "Well, the one positive thing about you not getting laid lately is that the stick is accurate. It would show up by now."

"I'm so glad you can find the silver lining in my celibacy."

"Come on, let's get you something light to eat, and then you need to go to bed."

She helps me stand from the toilet. "You want me to stay over tonight? I can crash on the couch."

I shake my head. "No, I'll be fine. Plus, the last thing you need is to get sick and then not be able to take care of your girls."

"Alright, well, you call me if you need anything."

She gets me a few Saltine crackers and a glass of Sprite

and then leaves me on the couch. After a few minutes, I surprisingly feel better.

I'm lost in thought but then jump at the sound of rattling in the front door. I know it's Evan because nobody else has a key.

I look up and see my handsome guy who looks like he hasn't slept in a month. His hair is disheveled, but he's no less sexy. He's still in his suit from work with my favorite light blue dress shirt of his.

"What are you doing here?" I croak out. I haven't seen him since he left, which makes this reunion even more painful.

"Your mom told me you were sick. I just wanted to check on you."

Of course, she did. My mother can't mind her own damn business.

"I'm fine."

"If you were fine, your mom wouldn't be watching Zoey."

I sigh. "I'm better now. I must have just caught a bug. I'll be good as new tomorrow."

He starts toward me, but then catches himself. I can tell he wants to touch me, but thinks better of it. I'm glad for that. I can't handle that tonight.

"Can I get you anything?" His eyes look so sad, and it rips me apart, but he's done this to us.

"No. Carly just left after bringing me Sprite and crackers."

He nods, and then there's an awkward silence between us. We've always found things to talk about, but right now, I don't know how to act around him.

I'm busy picking at the fuzz on the blanket on my lap when he interrupts my thoughts.

"Can I take you out once you're feeling better?" His words shock me. He wants to take me out? Like on a date?

"What?" I look up at him, and I'm sure he can read the confusion on my face.

"Yeah, I want to take you on a date. We can go wherever you'd like. Maybe talk a little." His uncertainty makes me want to cry, but there's no way I'm ready to even consider something like this.

"Please go," I say almost inaudibly. I don't know what else to say. I don't want to hurt him, but how dare he come in here like this after all these weeks.

He lets out a frustrated sigh. "Av, come on. I'm trying. Can you at least give me that?"

I shake my head. "I'm not ready. Can you give me that?" I shoot his words back at him.

"Fine. I'm going to the bathroom, and then I'll be out of your hair."

He leaves the room, and I wish I felt up to running to hide. I don't want to face him again before he leaves. It's so painful seeing him. I love that man like crazy, but sometimes that doesn't matter. Sometimes life gets in the way and things don't work out how we had hoped.

When I start feeling sick again, I lay back on the couch, but then hear the distinct sound of stomping coming from the hallway. *Great.*

"When were you going to tell me that you're pregnant?" He waves the empty pregnancy test box in the air." *Shit.* I completely forgot that was still in there, but I wasn't expecting him to come by tonight.

I carefully sit up, but this time, instead of being hit with nausea, I'm hit with anger.

"Don't worry. You're off the hook."

He sits in the chair across from me.

"What the fuck does that mean?" he roars, which makes me even angrier.

"I'm not pregnant!" I see the look of relief wash over his face. "Carly just wanted me to be sure after I spent the day throwing up. But don't worry, you won't have to be responsible for anyone else."

He shakes his head at me. "That's not what I meant and you know it. But if you're pregnant with my child, I would like to know."

"Well, I'm not, so you can go now."

He stands and then looks at me one last time.

"I'm really trying, Av." He pauses, and I can see the pain written on his face. "I didn't cheat on you."

The next second, I hear the door slam behind him and a picture fall off the wall.

How has this become our life?

33

AVERY

"Come on, Sleeping Beauty. Let's get you inside to Grams and Pops."

After much argument from my mother this morning, I reluctantly agreed to come to Sunday dinner at their house. I'm sure it mostly had to do with them both wanting to see Zoey, even though they see her every day during the week, but I know that they are both worried about the funk I've been in. If that's what you want to call it.

"There's my princess!" My mom shrieks as soon as we walk through the front door. My poor daughter startles in her carrier at her obnoxious tone. God love Lucy Giller, but she desperately needs a mute button sometimes.

I set the car seat on the floor and head toward the living room when my mom starts undoing Zoey.

"Hey, baby girl," my dad says as I enter the room. He stands from his recliner. My child has replaced me in my mom's eyes, but I'll always be a daddy's girl.

"Hey, Dad," I say into his chest as he wraps his strong arms around me.

"You doing okay?" He pulls back from our embrace and looks me in the eyes, searching for an answer.

"Yeah," I sigh. "I'm alright." He knows I'm lying but lets it go anyway.

"Good. Let's go in the kitchen and see what your mom is cooking up. I thought I smelled her famous oatmeal raisin cookies." He squeezes my hand and then pulls me toward the kitchen.

"Ed, look at this little girl," Mom says as she fluffs out Zoey's tutu dress. It's the most adorable dress she owns. I probably think that because it's sparkly and purple and reads *Mommy's Mini Me*. Claire bought it for her right after she was born, but she's just now able to fit into it.

"Hi Zo," Dad says as he takes her from Mom. He rubs her on the head and then kisses her cheek. She bats at his face when his whiskers rub against her.

"Ed, why don't you take her in the other room while me and Avery finish dinner?" She's trying not to be obvious, but I notice the look she gives Dad, telling him all that I need to know. She wants to talk to me in private, and I'm definitely not going to like whatever she has to say.

"Uh, sure. Let's go have some Pops and Zo time." It melts my heart every time I see the two of them together. She only has one set of grandparents, so it's important to me and Evan that she's always close to my parents.

They leave the room, and now, there's an awkward silence that surrounds the two of us.

Finally, I break the ice. "Alright, Mom. Why'd you really want me in here with you?"

She sets down her potholders and joins me at the table.

"Avery, you know me and your father both love you, but this has got to stop. What you and Evan have is very rare, and I'm sorry to say this, but you've taken your marriage for granted."

I gasp as I turn to look at her. "Excuse me? How have I taken my marriage for granted?"

She sighs. "Well, I think you need to at least try talking to him. What if you don't get another chance?"

At that, I sit up and eye her skeptically.

"What the hell does that mean?" I know she's going to scold me for cursing under her roof, but right now, I couldn't care less. I have no idea why she would say something like that to me.

"Avery Nicole, don't you curse at me in my house!" She tries to give me a dirty look, but it only makes me want to laugh.

"Sorry, Mom," I mumble at her like a child.

"You're forgiven. Now, what I mean is that you never know when you won't get another chance to tell him you love him." At that, I can feel the burn behind my eyes, caused by the tears that desperately need to come out.

"Avery, here you are upset over something silly when your friend will never have another chance to be mad at her husband, much less tell him how much she loves him."

The dam breaks, and I watch as the tears hit my arms that are resting on the table.

"He cheated on me."

She gasps, and out of the corner of my eye, I see her hand fly to her mouth. I've seemed to have stunned my mother silent.

"No. No, there's no way that man would do that to you."

"Mom, I wouldn't lie about something like this."

She doesn't have a chance to respond because Zoey starts crying from the other room. I'm thankful for the interruption.

"Ed, what did you do to that poor girl?" my mom hollers as she makes her way out of the kitchen.

I wipe at my eyes as I try to gather myself before going to my baby. Despite what's going on with me and her father, she needs me, and I need to keep myself together for her.

Once I've calmed down, I walk toward the living room where my mom is rocking my sweet baby girl. I hope she always knows how much Evan and I both love her, no matter what happens to our marriage.

"How's work going, princess?" my dad asks as he takes a bite of my mom's cheese bread. The stuff is seriously to die for.

I moan. "Ugh, it's going. Charlotte is driving me more crazy than usual, but I have a few new clients who have been fun to work with."

"Are they here in Phoenix?" my mother asks as she lifts her sweet tea to her lips.

"Yeah, mostly. But I still have that big one in Peoria."

I know that Evan always has hated that I've continued to work since having the baby, but now, I'm thankful I did. If I'm going to be a single mother, I need to have a full-time job.

"What kind of projects are they?" Dad asks.

I finish chewing my spaghetti before answering him. "Well, the big one is a couple who are expecting twins. They wanted us to transform their garage into a big nursery." I roll my eyes at the extremity of it all.

"People are ridiculous!" My mom shakes her head.

I just laugh. "I agree."

"Avery, have you thought about staying home with Zoey so you can spend more time with her?" Mom reaches over and grabs my hand. I want to pull away with irritation but decide against it.

God love my mother, but there are times when she does not have a filter. This would be one of those times.

"Mom, why do you have to keep bringing this up?" I wipe my mouth with my cloth napkin. Heaven forbid she purchase paper napkins. "Did you forget what I just told you?"

She ignores my question. "You know that I stayed home with you and your sister for many years while your dad worked. I have never regretted that."

Wow. That felt like a slap to the face.

"So, you think that because I'm a working mother that I'll regret not staying home with my child?" I shake my head and stand from my chair. "Dad, sorry to leave so soon, but I need to get Zoey home to bed."

He gives me a weak smile, but I know he understands.

"It's okay, sweetheart. Get her home, and we'll see you again soon." He stands and walks toward me and places a kiss on my cheek. "I'll talk to her," he says into my ear, and my chest tightens. I often feel like he's the only one in my corner. I've always been a Daddy's girl, but I need him more than ever right now.

"Thanks, Dad," I whisper and then turn to grab Zoey from my mother's arms.

"You don't need to act like this. You know we just worry about you." She leans in and kisses my daughter on the forehead before I take her.

"If you were really worried about me then you would know that I have to work because my husband and I will be getting a divorce."

Silence fills the room, and I leave without another word. It hurt to say, but they are nothing more than the truth.

I FINALLY GET Zoey to bed and head to the kitchen desperately needing to stop ignoring the overflowing dishes in the sink. I'm exhausted, but if I don't do them, I'm going to start attracting flies. My heart squeezes in my chest at the thought that Evan isn't in the other room watching E-Sports while I pick up the house.

Not liking the silence, I walk to the living room and switch the TV on to his favorite channel. I collapse into his recliner, and my face immediately goes into my hands as the tears start to fall, yet again. Will this ever get easier? I can't imagine the pain ever going away. I've loved that man for a long time. Despite what he's done, I don't think it'll ever be possible not to.

After what feels like hours, I make my way back to the dishes and get lost in thought as I load them into the dishwasher. This is something I've never minded doing because it's so mundane, but right now, I don't have energy to do anything.

I get lost in thought as I scrub the pizza pan. I can't even remember when I actually made a pizza last. I'm starting to disgust myself. I never imagined I'd find myself living like this.

My mind drifts to Evan, not that it's ever far from him. I wonder what he's doing at this very moment. I drop the dishrag into the soapy water and slide to the floor.

I'm jump when I hear keys rattling in the lock at the front door. I stand and head down the hallway on shaky legs. I know that it's not an intruder, but I'm not ready to face the person on the other side of the door, again.

I stand there with a deer-in-the-headlights look on my face, as the door slowly opens after it's unlocked.

He startles slightly when he sees me standing near him.

"Hey, Av." He gives me a weak smile, and I hate the sadness I see etched on his handsome face. His face is marred with a good week's worth of stubble. He never grows a full beard like this, so it takes me by surprise. He's always taken pride in his appearance, and this only makes my heart crack more. Why do I still feel this way after what he's put me through? After what he's done to our marriage?

When I don't say anything in return, he slowly walks toward me.

"I need to grab my navy suit for court tomorrow. Sorry if I scared you. I tried to call you but your phone went straight to voicemail."

"You mean to tell me that you couldn't come by the house when Zoey was awake so she could see her *father?*" I spit the words out with hatred in my tone. Hate is the furthest thing I feel for this man, but right now, I hate what he's doing to me and our family.

Anger fills his eyes.

"Avery, I just realized I didn't have the suit I needed. I wouldn't dare ask you to see my daughter in your presence."

He marches past me without another word. The urge to follow him is strong, but I resist and walk back to the kitchen instead.

I busy myself with the dishes but still when I hear footsteps behind me. I don't turn to look at him. It hurts so bad to see him like this, and it pisses me off that I feel that way. He deserves to be as miserable as I am.

Evan clears his throat. "Claire and Ryke are grilling out Friday night. I'd like to come get Zoey for it." He's not asking, not that he has to. She is, after all, his daughter too.

"Okay." Is all I say, and a moment later, I hear the front door pulled quietly shut. I drop the rag into the soapy water and rest my hands on both sides of the sink, my head hanging low. My heart is pounding, and it's only seconds later when the tears start falling again. One by one, mixing into the water.

I've always been a pretty content and outgoing person, but I hate that I've become this weak girl that I don't even recognize anymore.

34

AVERY

It's Monday morning, and I really don't want to go to work today. Actually, it's the absolute last place I want to be, after the shitty night I had. When I finally made it to bed, I couldn't get the image of his angry face out of my mind.

I walk to the kitchen to mix a bottle up for Zoey when I hear an insistent pounding on the front door.

Zoey is now screaming her head off, so I lift her out of her bed and put the bottle to her mouth. I decide against answering the door. I don't feel like dealing with anyone this morning. If it's someone important, they'll call if they need me.

Suddenly, the pounding starts up again, and I moan in frustration. I set Zoey in her chair, which has her screaming again. This better be important.

I look through the peephole and then sigh at the sight of my sister-in-law. I really hate that we've put her in the middle of our shit.

As soon as the door is open, I'm in her arms. I'm glad

that she's not mad at me over all of this. She makes her way into the living room and squats on the floor to kiss the top of Zoey's head, who has thankfully stopped crying.

"Is everything okay?" I'm worried that something is wrong if she is here so early. Typically, she would just call to check on me, not make an unplanned visit.

She stands and gives me a sympathetic look, and I don't like it one bit.

"I'm worried about you guys."

"He told you he stopped by, didn't he?"

She nods. "Yeah, but he didn't have to. He looked like shit when he got back to my house last night." She sits in the recliner. "Av, I don't think he cheated on you."

I lift Zoey out of her seat and then start to feed her again.

"Why was Mallory in his hotel room?" I'm sure she can hear the crack in my voice. I really don't feel like crying before I have to go to work. I've done enough of that over the past few weeks, to fill a damn river.

I look up at her and can see the hesitation on her face.

"What aren't you saying?" I prop Zoey up on my shoulder to burp her.

"He told me that after they went to the bar that night, she showed up at his door crying because her boyfriend had just broken up with her. She walked into his room uninvited." She waves a hand in the air. "Anyway, I don't remember it all, but he did tell me that she tried to hit on him, and when he dismissed her, she took her shirt off in front of him. But Av, he left and went to get another room. I didn't believe him at first either, because it looked terrible; her being in his room, but that's not like him at all."

I want to believe what she's telling me, but I don't know if I can. If it's not true, I risk putting my heart through the shredder again, and I won't allow myself to do that.

It hurts so damn much. I think that's why I haven't let him explain to me what happened. I'm worried about what he'll tell me. The heartache is unbearable.

Whatever the case, I know I want to strangle that bitch. I should have known from the first time that I met her, that she was no good. She had homewrecker written all over her perfect little face and fake ass boobs.

"He's your brother, you have to believe him," I mutter.

"No, I don't. I just know how much pain he's been in lately, and that's not how a man who cheats on his wife acts."

I stand to get Zo dressed.

"I've gotta get ready for work." I dismiss the conversation. I don't have time to dwell on this right now. I'll drive myself crazy all day if I think about it too long.

She stands and hugs me again.

"Yeah, okay. Ryke has to get to work too, so I better get home. I just wanted to check on you."

"Thanks, babe. Love you."

"Love you, too, sister. Call me later."

Needless to say, I don't make it to work on time. I spend a half hour on the floor of the shower, washing my tears down the drain. I know Claire is only trying to help, but now I feel worse than I did before. As much as I want to believe what she told me, I can't afford to let my walls down too easily.

"WHERE HAVE YOU BEEN? You look like shit." Leave it to Carly to comment on my disheveled appearance.

I sigh as I plop myself down into my desk chair.

"I had the shittiest morning possible and didn't even get to stop to get coffee. FYI, I will be a bitch today." I glare at her.

"Thanks for the heads up." She winks at me as she turns back to her computer.

After Claire's visit this morning, the baby had a nasty blow out in her diaper, and I had to give her a bath before we could walk out the door. I swear I have never seen so much poop in my life. I was late dropping her off with my mom, but then, of course, I had to explain to her what was going on because she wouldn't let me leave until she knew why I looked so upset.

"No, but really. What's going on with you?" She eyes me skeptically. "Have you talked to Evan?" She turns in her seat as she bites on the bottom of the pen she's holding.

"Yeah." I rub my hands over my face. After my long shower this morning, I didn't have time to put makeup on. I really do look like shit.

"That bad, huh?"

"Yeah, he came last night to pick up one of his suits, and we got into an argument."

I'm starting to get a headache, so I release my hair from the tight bun that it's in.

"Girl, I'm sorry," she says sympathetically.

"It's fine. But then Claire came over this morning and told me that she doesn't think he cheated on me."

"Do you believe her?"

I don't get to answer her because Charlotte's heels hitting the tiled floor interrupts us. I should have known I wouldn't get out of being late this easy.

"Avery, is there a reason you're late? *Again*," she asks in her bitchy tone. Usually, I'd be pissed, but today, I just roll my eyes as my back is toward her.

I decide I should probably face her while she's speaking to me in case her father is in the office this morning.

"I'm so sorry, Charlotte. I ended up having to give my daughter a bath before I could drop her off with my mother because she pooped all over her clothes," I say this in a sweet tone so she doesn't know that I'm being a bitch, but then she cuts me off.

"Say no more." She spins on her heels, and I hear, "Fucking disgusting."

Carly and I both chuckle.

"Damn, girl. You totally got her to shut the hell up quick. You're my new hero."

"Nobody wants to hear about baby shit, especially Cruella." We both laugh as we turn back to our computers.

"What are you up to tonight?" Carly spins in her chair to look at me. "Brad has Macy and Kaylee. I desperately need a drink. Why don't you join me?"

Going out and not having any responsibilities for a bit, sounds like just what I need.

"I'll have to talk to my mom to see if she can keep Zoey longer, but I'm in."

I turn back toward my work but then another thought crosses my mind.

"As long as we don't go to Ryke's."

"Deal. Let's go to The Blue Moon up on Gunder. Want to meet there?"

"Yeah, that sounds good."

Thankfully, the day goes a lot faster than I expected. I head home to change clothes and then realize that I haven't looked at my phone since I texted my mom about keeping Zoey longer this morning. I finally find it buried at the bottom of my purse and pull it out, seeing that I have two texts from Evan. My heart stills in my chest. After our argument last night, I'm scared to see what it says.

Evan: Hey Av, I know you're working but can you call me on your lunch break?

Evan: Look, I know you're upset with me and things aren't great with us right now, but if we can't talk, they never will be.

I know I'm avoiding the inevitable, but I'm really not ready to have another conversation with him yet.

I decide to shut my phone off and enjoy my night out with Carly. I'll worry about my shit storm of a life tomorrow.

✣ 35 ✣

AVERY

I arrive at The Blue Moon with minutes to spare before Carly is supposed to meet me. These days, it's rare that I'm early for anything. When I open the large door to the old brick building, I'm immediately hit with the scent of stale beer and cigarettes.

This place is way more crowded than I expected for a Monday night. The building is old with wood paneling throughout with no natural lighting. The large Bud Light chandeliers hang above the booths that outline all the walls. As soon as I find an empty spot, I notice that each tabletop is made out of melted down beer cans. In the center of the room, there are about a dozen pool tables, which are currently the cause of me not being able to hear myself think. This bar is different than most because the actual bar isn't in the center of the building, but tucked away in the back corner. As obnoxiously loud and smoky as it is in here, the place gives off a very unique vibe.

I check my phone and realize that Carly is ten minutes late. Deciding I don't want to wait any longer for a drink,

I slip my cardigan off and leave it in the booth so no one takes our table.

I go to the bar and order a beer and hop up onto a stool while I wait. I once again check my phone and notice that I have a text from her.

Carly: Sorry girl, I got held up at home. I'm on my way now.

I sit and nurse my beer, not wanting to get drunk tonight. Okay, I'm lying. I'd love to get drunk, but I have to be somewhat of a functioning adult tomorrow. Somedays, I wish that I could forget all responsibilities and take a vacation to a remote location. Just me and my Kindle. I know realistically that won't happen, but a girl can dream.

"Hey, chica!" Carly hollers, and I nearly jump out of my seat.

"Holy shit, woman. You about scared me to death."

"Sorry. Have you been here long?" She waves down the bartender, and once her order is in, she turns toward me.

"No, just a little while. I have a table over in the corner if you'd rather sit there. I just wanted a drink." I tilt my head back as I take the last sip of my beer.

"Good. So, I uh…" She starts but then looks unsure if she should go on.

"What?" I eye her skeptically.

"I have a date this weekend." She rushes out and then turns toward the bar when her drink is set in front of her.

"That's a good thing, right?" I ask, confused with the way she's acting.

"You aren't mad?" She slowly turns back to me.

"Why the hell would I be mad? I'm thrilled for you." I

reach toward her and wrap my arm around her in a half hug.

"I don't know. It's just with everything going on with you and Evan, I didn't want to upset you." I seriously hate that everyone feels like they have to walk on eggshells around me. I'm a freaking adult and know that just because me and my husband are having issues, doesn't mean that the rest of the world doesn't go on.

"Carly, seriously. I'm so happy for you. Who is it? Do I know him?"

"His name is Jed. He's a single dad from Macy and Kaylee's school." She blushes, and I have to admit it's adorable seeing her like this.

"That's awesome, Car!" I exclaim. "Do you need me to watch the girls while you go out?" It's nice to have anything to do that keeps my mind off Evan. I hate sitting around the house missing him. Especially when Zoey is sleeping, and I don't have anything to keep myself busy.

"They'll be with Brad, but thanks." She goes back to sipping her drink. "He's younger than me," Carly says without looking at me.

"Is that a problem?" I ask carefully. Surely, the guy can't be that much younger than her, especially if he has a kid at the same school as her girls.

"Uh, I'm not sure, but I'm guessing six or seven years younger." She fidgets with the label on her beer bottle.

"Carly, that's not that bad." I mean, Evan and I are the same age by just a few months, so I guess it is kind of weird, but in the grand scheme of things, it's not a big deal.

She clearly doesn't want to talk about this any longer,

so I order us each another drink, and then we head toward the table I had saved for us.

Deciding that we're both done drinking for the night, we go out to the dance floor. Not many people are out here dancing, so we act like carefree fools. It's nice since lately I've been anything but carefree. As we're bumping our hips together during some obnoxious teenybopper song, I feel someone's hand on my ass. I freeze before turning toward the asshole.

"Get your hand off my ass!" I yell like an idiot, clearly a little drunk. It's ridiculous that I can't even handle two beers.

The fucker continues to rub on my ass, and as I turn to deck the guy in the face, I instead come in contact with a hand.

What the...? I'm momentarily confused but then see Evan standing in front of me. A very *angry* Evan. I've never seen him like this before. What the hell is he doing here?

"Touch my wife again, I'll fucking kill you." He stares the guy down, and I'll admit I'm a little worried for him. "Avery, let's go," he says with a demanding tone, which has me even more pissed than the guy rubbing on my ass.

"No, I'm here with my friend. You don't need to rescue me, Evan." I turn around, trying to ignore him, but of course he isn't having it.

I go back to shaking my ass, ignoring the fact that Carly is giving me a concerned look.

I then feel a hot breath on the side of my face.

"Avery, now! We're leaving." *Oh, hell no.*

"Fuck off, Evan!" I know I'm making a scene, but how

dare he come in here acting like a control freak while I'm trying to have a fun night out.

I try to go back to dancing, but then I'm halted when he grabs me by the arm. He starts dragging me through the crowd, and I swat at him with my other hand like a two-year-old.

"Porter, everything okay here?" *Fuck.* Of course, the bouncer knows him, so I won't be getting any help from him.

"Yeah, man." He continues pulling me out of the bar.

By now, I'm pretty sure there's fire coming out of my eyes because I'm so angry with him.

"What the hell is wrong with you?" I scream in the middle of the sidewalk. Not caring that people are staring at us. He's the one who started this.

"What the hell is wrong with me? You're the one in there shaking your ass in front of all those dirty bastards. What the fuck are you doing here anyway?"

He's got me so worked up, I can hardly see straight.

"I was trying to enjoy a night out with my friend, until my dickhead husband decided to ruin that." I huff and throw my hands in the air. Then a thought hits me that makes me even angrier. "Wait a minute. What are you doing here? Were you following me?"

He doesn't answer me right away, which tells me that I'm right. He looks at me, carefully choosing his next words.

"Where's Zoey?" I can now see his irritation escalate. When his ears turn red, I know he's pissed.

I gasp. "Are you serious right now? She's at home sleeping." I roll my eyes at his ridiculousness. He's not impressed with my smart assery. "She's with my mother, if you must know."

I can tell he's biting his tongue, but he doesn't respond.

"I'm taking you home, and we're going to talk." He grabs my arm again, but this time not as rough as before. I know there's no use arguing with him because I'm not going to win this one.

Once I'm in the Jeep, I shoot Carly a quick text, not going into details. Although, it's possible that she heard our argument from inside the loud bar.

36

EVAN

The drive back to the house is unusually uncomfortable. I know she's mad, but I can't say I regret going to The Blue Moon tonight. My co-worker Simon texted me tonight telling me he saw her sitting at the bar by herself, and I was worried she'd get trashed and not be able to get home. I know she's smart, but I still didn't want to risk something happening to her. Then when I walked in and saw that douchebag with his hands all over her, I about came unglued. I did feel a sense of pride though when I heard her yelling at him, and then she tried to punch him but instead came in contact with my hand. I knew she'd be pissed when she saw me, but I couldn't bring myself to care. It doesn't matter that we're separated. She's still mine. And if I have any say, she'll be mine for the rest of our lives.

I pull into the driveway, and she's quick to unbuckle her belt and tries to dart out the door, but I grab her arm.

"Thanks for the ride," she grumbles, trying to get away from me.

"Av, stop," I say sternly, but I'm trying not to sound like a complete ass again.

"Stop what, Evan? Stop being pissed that you found the need to follow me? Why is that alright?" She's breathing heavily, and I have to admit I'm a little terrified at the possibility of her reaching across the armrest and slapping me in the face. Fuck, I don't care though. If it makes her feel better and I get the chance to talk to her, she can do whatever she wants to me. Although I'd prefer if she did other things to me. *Damn it, Porter. Get your mind out of the fucking gutter.*

"I wasn't following you. Simon was out with his wife and saw you at the bar. I just wanted to make sure you made it home safe." *It's the truth.*

"Whatever." She crosses her arms over her chest, pouting like a child, but I have to admit that it's damn adorable. "I'm going to bed." She reaches for the handle, but I stop her again.

"We need to talk." I'm not asking her because I know she wouldn't agree to it. She'll eventually cave though because she knows I won't leave until I get my way.

I finally let her leave the car and then wait a few seconds before I follow behind her. I know I'm going to have to play my cards right if I want her to listen to me. I'm stubborn, but my wife is even more stubborn than I am.

As I'm walking onto the porch, she slams the screen door shut, not bothering with the other door because she knows I'm behind her.

"I'm going to bed," she says again, starting down the hallway that leads toward our room, but like hell am I letting her walk away from me.

"Av, stop," I say louder than I mean to, but my frustration seems to be getting the best of me. She freezes at my words, and I'm sure the tone I'm using with her. I can see the hairs standing up on the back of her neck. "Talk to me."

She flips around so fast it takes me by surprise.

She gets up in my face, and I want so desperately to reach out to her and run my hands through her hair and then kiss her tempting lips, but I restrain myself. I haven't kissed her in weeks, and I'm sure she wouldn't respond to that well, especially not right now.

"No, Evan! I will not stop. I'm fucking sick of this. Please. Just go." She tries to walk away from me again, but I grab her shoulder and spin her back toward me. I can tell she's shocked by my actions.

I step away from her, knowing she most likely wants space.

"Avery," I say sternly. "I. Did. Not. Sleep. With. Her." Each word comes out clipped. I know I'm being an ass, but I'm done being nice. She won't listen to me, and I'm fucking tired of it. I don't know how else to get her to believe me. I throw my head back in frustration and yank at my hair. "I didn't sleep with anyone. No one, but you."

A single tear rolls down her beautiful face. I want her to believe me, but I can tell that she doesn't.

"Please go," she whispers.

"No." I shake my head. "I'm done letting you push me away. You know me better than anyone else. How could you think I'd do such a horrible thing to you?"

She wipes at the wetness on her face, and when she pulls her hands away, I can see the rage radiating off of her.

She chuckles. "Gee, I don't know. Maybe because I called your fucking hotel room and that bitch answered."

"I swear to God, it wasn't what you think."

She rolls her eyes and then turns her back on me.

I throw my arms up in the air in defeat.

"You know what? Fuck it." She pauses, but doesn't turn to look at me. "I thought you knew me better than that, but obviously, you think I'm a cheater *and* a liar. I'll just make this easier on you." I walk to the door, but before I open it, I say, "I'll have the divorce papers drawn up and sent to you. Let me know where you want to meet up to discuss custody."

As soon as the words come out of my mouth, I regret them, but I'm tired of this shit. Besides opening the door of my hotel room for that bitch, I did nothing wrong. Obviously, I'll never get it through her head that I didn't cheat on her.

When I pull the door shut behind me, I hear something crash against it from the other side, and then I hear her scream.

I don't think before I push the door back open, and I see her sitting against the wall, her knees pulled to her chest.

I'm careful not to step on any glass as I make my way to her.

"Are you okay?"

I look around the room and notice that the offending object was one of our wedding pictures.

"Everything was so perfect. How did we get here?" she asks in a whisper as she rocks back and forth.

I sigh as I sit across from her.

"It wasn't perfect, but we always knew how to get through things together. We also trusted each other."

She gasps at my words. I know they were harsh, but they're true.

I stand from the floor and then carefully clean up the glass before leaving my crying wife.

Do I want a divorce? Fuck, no, I don't. But I also know that I can't stay in a marriage with someone who can't trust me or who isn't willing to work things out with me.

I need a goddamn drink.

"Hey!" Sierra hollers as she answers the door of the beach condo she shares with her grandmother.

"Hey, Sier!" I hug my friend, and we both start crying. We've both been through a hell of a year. Hers, obviously way worse than mine, but we both need this time together.

Me and Zoey just flew into Carolina Beach Airport this afternoon. After Evan told me he'd be serving me with divorce papers last week, I booked a flight. I needed to get as far away from Phoenix as I could.

I haven't heard from him since, but I was hoping that I wouldn't before I left. His words hurt me like a knife to the chest, but I guess he was right. We should be able to trust each other. *What the fuck happened to our marriage?*

"Oh, my goodness, Av, she's gorgeous," Sierra says as she takes Zo from me.

I look behind her at Jayce.

"Look at little man! He is so stinking cute." I leave Sierra and Zoey at the front door and lift Jayce out of his seat. "Hi, sweet boy." I kiss his cheek, and my heart breaks all over again for Sier and both these little boys. Miles was a good husband and dad. I don't understand why something so terrible had to happen to such a great family.

"You must be Avery." I turn at the sound of a sweet, old voice. The woman is probably a good six inches shorter than me with a head full of white curly hair. I can definitely tell that she and Sier are related.

"I am." I smile at her as I walk her way. "You must be Grandma Rose."

The sweet older woman smiles at me and then pulls me into a hug.

"I am. Please make yourself at home. I've cleared out the guest room for you and your baby. Anything you need, just let me know."

I nod at her, and then she leaves me to go see Zoey, who is giggling away in Sierra's arms.

After we spend time with each other's kids, Grandma Rose pours us each a glass of her homemade sweet tea and tells us she'll keep an eye on the three of them while we sit on the back porch.

"It is so gorgeous here," I say as I sit in a lounger, looking out at the beautiful, sapphire blue Atlantic. "It's already blazing hot back home. Girl, I hate summer."

She chuckles. "Move here. It's always nice." She sips on her tea.

I sigh. "I'd love to live on the beach, but Phoenix is home." As soon as the words come out, I regret them. "I'm sorry, Sier." It was her home for a long time too, and I don't want to make her feel bad for leaving.

She waves me off. "Girl, don't apologize. It's been nice being close to Grandma Rose and my brothers. I honestly don't think I could ever leave now. Phoenix holds too many memories, you know?" I don't miss the single tear that falls down her cheek.

I jump out of my chair. "Scooch," I say as I sit next to her. "Come here." I wrap my arms around her, and she immediately starts to cry. I have a feeling she hasn't done enough of this lately. She's had to be strong for her boys.

She pulls away and then looks up at me. "Thanks." She sniffs. "I needed that."

I smooth out her black hair that has gotten longer since I saw her last.

"You don't have to thank me. I'm always here for you, sister girl."

She shakes her head. "I shouldn't be burdening you with this right now. You have your own stuff going on." She squeezes my hand. "You doing okay?"

"You're never burdening me. But yeah, I'm okay." I give her a small smile, but I know she isn't buying my lie.

"Avery Porter, don't lie to me. You can talk to me."

I sigh and throw my head back. "He told me last week that he's going to have divorce papers sent to me." It hurts to say the words, but not as much as hearing Evan say them.

"What?" She gasps. "I thought you said he's been begging you to talk to him. Why would he say that?"

I look up at the blue sky. It's so gorgeous here. I could definitely get used to this.

"He's upset that I don't trust him."

"Do you trust him?"

I rub at my eyes. I'm exhausted after traveling all day with a baby.

"I want to trust him, but I'm scared," I admit.

She stands from the chair we're sharing and positions herself so she's facing me and then grabs both my hands.

"Av, I've never in all my life seen a man look at a woman the way Evan does you." I feel the burn behind my eyes from the tears needing to fall. I've been a damn mess lately, and I hate it. I don't want to cry anymore.

"What have I done? I can't lose him."

She shakes her head. "You haven't done anything. You guys have been under a lot of stress lately. Av, I think that any woman, no matter how strong her marriage, would have thought the same thing you did."

I cover my face with my hands as soon as the tears finally get loose. I don't know if I'll be able to fix this.

"You need to talk to him."

It seems simple enough, but it scares the shit out of me. The thought of him rejecting me after I've pushed him away for so long, sends my emotions into a complete tailspin. I don't know if he could ever forgive me.

She gives me a small smile. "It's understandable that you're scared, but that man loves you, Av. He's been trying to get you back. Show him that you trust him."

"What if it's too late?"

"It's not. I'm sure of it. He was just pissed, Avery, just like you were. I'm sure he didn't mean anything about wanting a divorce."

"I've really fucked up."

"No. You just need to get him back now. I have no doubt in my mind that he'd take you back in a heartbeat. And I have no doubt in my mind that when you talk to him, you'll have wild and crazy monkey sex."

This makes me laugh. "You really think so?" When I see the Cheshire grin on her face, I correct myself. "I mean the part about him taking me back, although wild and crazy monkey sex sounds nice too."

"Definitely." She smiles. "Why don't you take some time for yourself this week, and once you get home, go get your man back."

I don't know if what she's suggesting is going to be that simple, but I nod my head in agreement.

We spend the rest of the day on a much lighter note. Sierra and Grandma Rose take me to see their beachside bakery, Rosie Posey's. It's a cute little shop that has every sweet imaginable. Grandma Rose opened it when she retired here, but Sierra has since taken it over. I'm glad that she has something to keep her busy, not that her boys don't already.

"Ohmigod!" I exclaim when I take a bite out of the decedent lemon tart. "This is incredible! Sier, you made this?"

She nods with a smile on her face. "Yeah, Grandma Rose has taught me everything she knows since I moved here."

"Can we just hang out here the rest of the week?" I'm pretty sure I'm going home forty pounds heavier, but I don't care. This stuff is delicious.

After reluctantly leaving the bakery, they take us down the beautiful boardwalk. The ocean is breathtaking and definitely something I could get used to seeing every day. As much as I love the weather, I made sure I brought a jacket for both me and Zoey. It's a good twenty-five degrees cooler here than it is back home. I'd love to spend the summer here instead of in the fiery desert, but that's where my guy is. After our conversation earlier, I feel much better, but I'm still worried about what he'll say to me. I'm not naïve, I know that things aren't going to magically get better, but I also know that they never will if I don't put any effort in.

I'm lost in thought when I feel Sier wrap her arm around me.

"Hey, you okay?"

I nod. "I'm perfect."

The words aren't completely true, but I'm hoping that soon, they will be.

38

EVAN

I pull into Claire and Ryke's driveway, parking my Jeep off to the side. Today was a day from hell at work, and I want nothing more than to drink my ass off and then pass out. Although, that's probably not the smartest move, considering I have to be at the courthouse early as shit tomorrow. I find that working late keeps my mind off my girls a little longer. I mean, they always find a way to slip into my mind throughout the day, but at least I can focus on something else for a bit. At the thought of my wife, I get a pain in my chest. I take a few calming breaths before getting out.

I unlock the front door and immediately hear a familiar sound. *Zoey.* What the hell is she doing here? Not that I'm not happy about seeing my daughter, but I would have left work sooner had I known she was here.

I walk to the other side of the house where all the bedrooms are and finally find my screaming baby rocking with my sister in Aria's room. I walk toward them and, without asking, sweep her out of Claire's arms.

"What's the matter, baby girl?" I coo into her ear, and she starts to calm down a bit. I like to think that has something to do with me. She is a Daddy's girl after all. I turn and look at my sister, and I'm sure she can see the annoyance on my face. "How long has she been here, and why didn't you tell me?"

She sighs as she stands from the rocking chair. "She's been here since Lucy brought her around four. She had errands she had to run, so I said I'd watch her." Avery is off work at three-thirty, so this isn't making any sense.

"Where is my wife?" I roar and immediately feel bad because now my daughter is crying in my arms again. I try to soothe her by rubbing her little back.

"First off, calm your ass. Don't come in my house yelling at me." Damn, she's about as feisty as Avery. "Second of all, Avery had to work late, so she's still at the office." *God damn it.* I hate that she works there at all, but that place isn't safe at night. She's smack dab in the middle of downtown Phoenix, and I've seen enough crazy shit over the years from being an attorney. I've told her numerous times that I didn't want her working there late, but hell if she ever listens to me. Why would she?

"Fuck," I murmur. "Alright, well, she appears to be hungry, so I'm going to make her a bottle. Where's her bag at?" I start walking out of the room with my daughter.

"It's in the front room on the couch."

I find Zoey's bag and set her in Aria's seat so I can fix her a bottle. No matter what happens with Avery and I, I will always be the best damn father that I can be. God, the thought of losing my wife makes me fucking nuts.

I had to find out through my sister that her and Zoey were going out to North Carolina to see Sierra. I was a little pissed, but at the same time thought maybe it would be good for her to clear her mind a bit. I, of course, never had divorce papers made up. I'm not planning on it either. If she wants to be done for good, she can do it, but she's going to hear me out before I sign a damn thing.

"Hey, man," Ryke says as he enters the kitchen. I run the bottle under hot water to heat it up a little. Zoey will only be unhappier if it's cold.

"Hey," I mumble and know right away that he's going to ask what's crawled up my ass. Ever since moving in with him and Claire, we've gotten closer. I have other friends, but it's different when you live with someone, and I can only tell my sister so much.

"What's wrong with you? Your daughter is in the other room. I thought you'd be happy to see her." Great. Now I feel like shit.

I huff as I mix the nasty-smelling powder into the water. "Of course, I'm happy to see my daughter, fucker. Some of us don't have perfect little lives like you, Ryke."

Shit, that probably wasn't the best thing to say. *Open mouth, insert foot.*

"I'm going to let that slide because you're in a pissy mood, but you know that neither me or your sister have always had it easy. We've had to work hard for what we have now."

And I know that's the truth. Between him being cheated on by his ex and all the shit with Trevor Davis, they've been through hell and back. But that doesn't make me feel any better.

I walk into the living room to find Claire holding Zoey on the couch, who has thankfully stopped crying. I hate seeing her so upset.

"You want me to feed her?" my sister asks.

"No, I'll do it." I lift her into my arms. I need a part of my life back, and if being with my daughter is all I get right now, I'll take it.

"Are you pissed that I agreed to watch her?"

I look up from my daughter who is guzzling her bottle like she hasn't eaten in years.

"What? Why would I be pissed about that?"

She raises her eyebrows at me. "I know you hate that she works at the shit hole, but I wanted to see my niece."

"No, I'm not pissed." I shake my head. "When did they get back from Sierra's?"

Zoey is starting to drift to sleep, so I put her in the portable bed Claire has set up in the living room, after kissing the top of her head. "Daddy loves you, baby girl."

"Just last night. I was surprised she went back to work so soon."

"I'm not," I mutter under my breath.

"Bro, you have got to stop with the macho asshole shit. *That* will not win her back."

I give a sarcastic chuckle. "I'm pretty sure nothing will help me get her back, so what difference does it make?"

She stands when she hears Aria crying from the other room. I'm guessing Avery will be here soon, and she won't be thrilled to see me. Oh well. I live here. What does she expect?

Ryke goes to relieve Claire in the nursery, and she plops back down on the couch. I stare at her, trying to find the words to say.

"How could she think I'd do this to her? To our family?"

"Ev, it looked really bad. I love Ryke, but the same

thing happened with us when we were dating, remember?" I do remember that. His ex tried causing them problems. Weird thing is, now Claire is friends with her.

I nod. "Yeah, I do remember that."

"I loved him, but it still looked really bad. Monica was trying to hurt us, just like Mallory was trying to do." She gives me a sympathetic smile. "I really can't blame her, Evan. She loves you, and the thought of losing you to another woman, hurt her." She pauses, so I can digest her words. "You have to remember that she just had a baby and is probably feeling a bit insecure right now."

"Goddamn it." She's right. I hate that our marriage has come to this. I just want things to be how they were before all this shit went down. I miss her so fucking much.

"Being in a marriage with the right person is one of the best things that can ever happen to a person, but you still have to work at what you want." She leans her head on the back of the couch, staring up at the ceiling before she goes on. "Don't give up on her."

Without responding, I stand from the chair and lift my sleeping daughter into my arms. I carry her to Aria's room, where Claire has a second crib set up for her.

I want nothing more than to be at home with my two girls. I just have to figure out a way to get her to understand that I'm not the asshole she thinks I am. Well, I am, but I'm the asshole that loves her more than fucking anything. So much it hurts.

I kiss the top of Zoey's head that smells of her lavender bath soap. Avery said it's supposed to help her sleep better at night. Damn, maybe I should use some of that because I haven't slept for shit lately.

After gently laying her down, I walk back toward my sister.

"How do I fix this?" I ask as I drop into the recliner and kick my feet up. I could really use a beer about now.

"Bro, there's nothing you can do until you both decide to stop being stubborn asses." Her phone rings from the other room, so she starts to get up. "You two are the most bull-headed people I've ever met, and how you haven't managed to kill each other yet is beyond me." She walks toward the kitchen but turns around before leaving the room. "But I've never known two people who were more in love than you guys." At that, she leaves me in my thoughts. She's right. I love her more than anything. You hear about people splitting up because they've stopped loving each other. Well, that's definitely not us. Since the day I met her, I've never stopped loving her.

"Oh, God." I hear my sister cry, so I immediately run to see what's wrong.

The look on her face tells me that something is seriously wrong.

"We'll be there soon."

She ends the call, and my world momentarily stops at her next words.

39

AVERY

"God, I'm fucking exhausted," Carly says behind me as I shut down my computer. It's nearing nine o'clock at night, and we're just now leaving. Zoey and I flew home last night from North Carolina, and I should have taken the day off. "Why did Cruella get to leave before us? Such a bitch," she mumbles, which has me giggling.

"This actually surprises you?" I ask as I grab my Louis Vuitton bag from under my desk.

"No, but I don't understand how one person can be so evil."

"How long have you worked here?" I ask sarcastically as we head for the elevator.

"Six years. You know this."

"That's my point, biotch. Was Charlotte Kinsley not malicious when you started all those years ago?" We both know that there's no possible way that the woman has ever shown any kind of concern for anyone but herself. It's really no wonder that she's still single at nearly forty.

"Well, she definitely wasn't this bad. I swear she has gotten worse in her old age." We both burst out with laughter, knowing that Charlotte would have a coronary if she ever heard anyone refer to her as being old.

I can't stop laughing. "Can you imagine if she heard you say that?"

"I'm totally going to say that shit to her whenever I decide to leave this hell hole."

I look at her and give her my best glare. "You are not allowed to leave until I do. You're one of the only ones around here that I can halfway tolerate."

She smacks me in the arm at my smart remark. "Whatever. Fuck you."

"Hey, Marie. We're the last ones here. We'll see you tomorrow," I say to the receptionist at the front desk. She's a sweet older lady with a head full of white hair. She's probably old enough to be mine and Carly's grandmother. His daughter may not have a nice bone in her body, but at least Mr. Kinsley makes sure that security walks her down to her car when she has to stay late. I personally think it's shit that they make her work so many hours, but I never hear her complaining about it. God, I hope I'm not still working here when I'm her age.

She smiles up at both of us. "Could one of you help me get a box from the top shelf in the supply room before you go?"

"Sure, I can do that," Carly says and then turns toward me, "go ahead and go. I know you need to pick Zoey up from Claire's."

"You sure?" We never used to walk to our cars alone, but now, there are high-end security cameras everywhere.

"Yeah, I'll be right behind you. Go." She waves me off with her hand.

"Alright, I'll see you tomorrow." I give her a half hug and wave goodbye to Marie.

What Carly doesn't know is that I'm planning on seeing Evan tonight and asking him to go somewhere with me so we can talk. I'm nervous as hell, but it's time to talk to my husband. I'm still scared, but I feel like a bitch for ever thinking that he was capable of cheating on me. That's not him at all. He'd never do something like that to me, and the fact that I felt that way for so long, makes me feel like shit. Will he even be willing to talk to me after the way I've acted? Hell, I don't know if I'll be able to handle the rejection. What if he's waiting for me with divorce papers in his hands? I shake the thought out of my mind. If I let myself get stuck in my head, I'll be a chicken shit and never talk to him. That's not even an option. We need him back.

I walk to the elevator and push the button for the lower level. I hate being here this late, but I'm sure I'm leaving early compared to other people in the building. There're all sorts of offices here, and I'm not even sure what all of them are for.

"Have a good night, Mrs. Porter."

"You too."

I push through the door that leads out to the parking lot after smiling at George, the security guard who always stands inside the entrance to the building.

Once I make it to my car, I reach into my purse to retrieve my keys. The light above my BMW is out, so I can hardly see anything. I hit unlock on the key fob and then tense at the touch of a hand on my back. *What the...?*

I have no idea who's behind me and don't have a chance to look because in the next moment a cool material is being placed over my eyes. It's tied tight, almost painfully. *What the hell is going on right now?*

I start to scream, but then I'm cut off when something is placed in my mouth, silencing my cries.

Next, my wrists are grabbed roughly, and I'm being dragged away from my car, but I can't tell where I'm going, as I can't see. I'm trying to pull away, but of course, it's pointless because this person has a good grip on me. I have no idea what is going to happen to me.

Thoughts of my husband and daughter flash through my mind. What if I never get to tell Evan that I'm sorry or have one last time to tell him that I love him? I'm going to die with him hating me. Tears prick at the back of my eyes.

Now, I'm pushed up against what feels like a pole. It's cool on my exposed skin. I feel my wrists being tied to it, then in the next second, my hair is being yanked, and I'd be surprised if half of it wasn't just pulled out of my head.

Pain. So much pain. I think I'm going to pass out.

I start to slide down the pole, no longer able to stand, not thinking about what could happen to me. The pain in my head is causing a ringing in my ears.

The worst comes when a foot connects with my ribs and then my face.

There's no way I'm going to make it out of here alive.

I'm so tired. I can't keep my eyes open a moment longer.

❦ 40 ❦

EVAN

"I need to see my wife, Avery Porter." I demand when I get to the front desk in the emergency room.

The young girl with short, curly hair, with a name tag that reads 'Shelly,' gives me a deer-in-the-headlights look. She appears to have no clue about what she's supposed to be doing, but I don't care right now. I just need to see my wife.

"You'll have to have a seat, sir. I'll find out where she is."

I can feel the veins starting to pop out of my head, and I'm sure that my face is turning several shades of red. I don't fucking have time for this.

I see Claire running through the doors in the next second, worry written all over her face.

She rushes up to me, out of breath. "What did you find out?" She bends over, grabbing her knees.

"Not a damn thing." I throw myself into a chair. I feel so useless. For all I know, she could be on her deathbed right now, and I'm stuck in this fucking room until someone conveniently finds the time to update us.

We wait for what feels like hours, but it's probably only been five or ten minutes.

"Mr. Porter?" I hear the girl behind the desk call. Claire and I are out of our seats in record time.

"Can we see her?" I have no idea what kind of shape she's in. All we know is that some low-life fucker beat the shit out of her in the parking lot at her office. This is my biggest fear unfolding right in front of me, and I'm powerless to do anything about it.

She stands from her chair and comes to stand in front of us. "Dr. Norton said you can go to the fourth floor where your wife is in a room, and he will be up to update you shortly." I sigh in relief, although I'm not sure I'm going to feel the same once I see her.

She walks to the sliding doors and enters a password into the keypad, and they slide open.

"The elevator is to your right, and she's in room 407."

Without letting her say anything else, Claire and I are sprinting to the elevator. I push the up button, silently willing it to open. Thankfully, we only wait a few seconds before it dings, telling us that a car is waiting to take us up.

Once inside, I look over at my sister who has tears in her eyes. I lean my head against the wall and stare up at the numbers as each one lights up, indicating what floor we're on. What if she doesn't pull through this? What if I never get another chance to tell her I love her and apologize for being an ass? *Fuck.* I need her. Our daughter needs her. I can't even begin to fathom a life without her in it.

We finally stop at the fourth floor, and we turn down the hallway, but a young nurse sitting behind the nurse's station stops us.

"Sir, may I help you?" If this girl tries to stop me, I'm going to blow a gasket. Why is it so fucking hard to just let me get to her?

"No, I just need to get to my wife, Avery Porter." I continue down the hallway, but then I'm halted by Claire when she puts her hand on my arm.

"Evan, maybe she'll let us talk to the doctor before we go see her." I really don't want to talk to anyone else, but I guess she has a point. At least he would prepare me for what I'm about to see on the other side of the door at room 407.

I pull at my hair. "Yeah, alright."

I walk back to the nurse. "Will Dr. Norton be up soon?"

"Yes, he just called and said he's on his way."

It is taking all my restraint not to run to Avery's room. I need to see her. I need to know that she's going to be alright.

"Mr. Porter?" An older man with black hair with patches of white throughout looks at me with sympathy in his eyes. I don't want anyone's fucking sympathy.

"Yes, can you tell me what's going on with my wife?" At this point, I feel like I've hit a dead end. I feel like a hamster running in one of those balls. No matter how fast they go, they never actually get anywhere. Yeah, that's me right now. I know that any minute now the adrenaline is going to wear off, and I'm going to crash from exhaustion.

"Come sit down." He gestures toward the waiting room.

"No, I'm fine here."

He nods in understanding. "Alright, your wife was injured pretty severely tonight. She has a severe concussion, a broken nose, and two broken ribs." I know he's still talking to me, but I can't seem to hear him from the buzzing in my ears. As soon as I find out who did this to her, they're dead.

"Motherfucker!" I'm sure every patient on the floor just heard me yell, but right now, I can't bring myself to care.

"She's going to be alright though. She's been sleeping, but she's conscious, so as soon as she wakes up you can visit with her. She was a bit confused, so she might not remember what happened to her, but I'm confident that she won't have any permanent damage."

I release the breath I didn't realize I was holding.

"Follow me, I'll take you to see her."

"I'll let you have some time with her first," Claire tells me and then heads toward the waiting room.

I follow the doctor down the hallway.

He pushes the door open, but before I enter, I take a deep breath.

"You coming, son?" the doctor asks when I don't follow him.

"Yeah, I just need a minute." I pull tight at my hair as I lean my back up against the wall. I'm relieved to know that she's going to be alright, but I know that as soon as I see her battered body, I'm going to want to go find the sick fuck who did this to her and murder them with my own two hands.

I finally feel a little calmer, so I walk into the room. I'm greeted with the sounds of monitors beeping, and I'm hoping that it's a good sign. Dr. Norton passes me, telling me he'll be back to check on her again soon. I round the corner, and my breath nearly hitches in my throat. My beautiful girl lays on the bed with her eyes closed.

Her right eye is purple and swollen, and she has stitches above her eyebrow. Her nose is wrapped in tape, and I can see dried blood in her hair. Whoever the fucker is who did this to her, just messed with the wrong family. I feel like I'm going to be sick.

As I'm staring at her, I'm thrown from my stupor when she wakes up crying uncontrollably.

In an instant, I'm by her side. "Shh. Shh. It's okay, Av. I'm here." I hold her in my arms the best I can while I'm bent over the side of the bed and gently rub her head, careful not to touch any of her injuries. I feel like someone has just pulled my heart out of my chest and stomped on it. I can't handle seeing her like this.

"Ev?" she rasps out once she's fully awake.

"I'm here. You're safe. I promise," I say soothingly into her ear.

She starts to cry again, the sight of her like this is enough to bring me to my knees.

I pull a chair up next to her bed and get as close to her as I can. "I'm so sorry. I'm so, so sorry," I whisper and then realize that my own tears have begun to mix with hers.

I hear a nurse come in, most likely to check her vitals, but she leaves after we both ignore her.

We pull away from each other, and she stares up into my eyes.

"Where's Zo?"

"She's with Ryke at their house sleeping." I smile at her.

"Did you get to see her tonight?" As much as we've

been fighting, I know she's glad that I've continued to see our daughter, but I want to be able to see both my girls at every possible moment.

"Yeah, I did. I fed her and got to snuggle with her a bit." I sigh, and know the emotion is raw in my voice.

"Oh, sweetheart!" We both turn toward the sound of Avery's mom as she enters the room. I'm guessing Claire called her, because honestly, that was the last thing on my mind.

"Hey, Mom." Lucy stares down at her as tears stream down both of their faces, and then she leans down to grasp her into a tight hug. I want to say something but think better of it. Avery seems to be fine, and getting on my mother-in-law's bad side is the last thing I want to do tonight.

As much as I want to be here with my wife, I think she needs rest, and I'm not sure if she wants me here right now.

Once both Avery and Lucy are done crying, I walk back to the bed and rest my hand on her shoulder. "Hey, I'm going to take off so I can get back to Zoey. Are you alright with your mom?"

I know it's a shitty excuse, but I'm really not sure what I'm supposed to do right now. The overprotective asshole in me wants to tell her that I'm staying no matter what she wants, but I can't do that to her. Not after everything she's been through tonight.

I immediately see the pain radiating off her beautiful face.

"Oh, okay." She turns her head away from me and stares at the busy traffic outside the hospital window.

"Hey, you alright?" I gently rub her arm.

She slowly turns to look at me, and now, she's once again crying. This time, I'm the cause. *God damn it.*

Lucy walks out of the room, apparently realizing we need privacy.

"Please, don't go," she whispers up at me, and I know that there's no way in hell I can leave her.

"You sure?" I search her eyes for any doubt she might have, but come up empty. "I wasn't sure if you'd want me here."

"I want you here. Please?" Her voice is pleading, even though she knows that I'd do anything for her. "I- I'm scared."

"I'm not going anywhere."

EVAN

I've been staring at the damn TV for the last three hours. Yes, three long, agonizing hours. Avery was released this afternoon from the hospital, but as soon as we got home, she locked herself in our bedroom and hasn't come out since. I had Claire run to the pharmacy so I wouldn't have to leave her, not that she's letting me do anything for her anyway.

She thankfully agreed to letting me take care of her since she has to be supervised, but she really hasn't been herself. Not that I expect anything less, after everything she's been through in the last twenty-four hours.

Getting bored of just sitting, I get up and head to the kitchen. I know I've got some beer in here that I bought before leaving. Avery doesn't like what I drink, so I'm not surprised when I see that it's still in the fridge. I pop the cap off and take a long swig, letting it burn my throat as it goes down. I need something to help calm my nerves. It felt like we were having a breakthrough at the hospital last night, but now, she's shut down. The attack really did a number on her emotionally. The doctor she saw in the hospital, recommended therapy. I refuse to leave her side until we know who the hell is behind the shit she went through last night. Although, I'm hoping she doesn't make me leave at all. I need to be here with my family.

My phone rings in my pocket. I take one last swig and then set my beer on the counter before answering it. It's my detective buddy Anthony from the Phoenix PD.

"Hey, man. Any news?" I had called him this afternoon before we left the hospital, needing to get answers. Avery was my first concern, so I didn't do anything about it last night.

He sighs heavily. "No. Man, this is going to be near impossible because the jackass clearly knew what he was doing. They found all the cameras before approaching Avery. He definitely wasn't dumb about this."

"God damn it." I hope I didn't just wake Avery. As much as I want to talk to her, she needs rest more. "So, what do we do now?"

"Tomorrow, the PD is sending five officers to the Horton Building and we're going to start questioning other people who may have been there around the time she left. Not to say that it was one of her co-workers, but we can't rule that out right now." He pauses, and I hear typing in the background. "You said her friend found her, right?"

"Yeah, Carly Weston." Carly came to the hospital last night practically in hysterics. Avery told her several times that it wasn't her fault, but she was very difficult to console.

"Okay, that might help us."

"Sounds good. Let me know whenever you hear anything."

"Will do. Just focus on getting your wife better, and we'll do the rest."

"Thanks, man. I appreciate it."

We hang up, and I grab my hair in frustration. This is such a fucking shit storm.

I'm exhausted, so I decide to call it a night and try to get a little sleep before Avery wakes. I'm sure it'll be pointless even trying because my mind is going a mile a minute, but neither of us slept well at the hospital. She woke up several times crying, so of course, I couldn't fall back to sleep after that.

I didn't bring anything from Claire's, and my clothes I do have here are locked up with my wife, so I strip out of what I'm wearing and lay on the couch in only my boxers.

I grab a throw pillow and set it behind my head. I stare out at the dark sky, knowing that I won't be seeing much of the back of my eyelids tonight. Sleeping has been near impossible since I left on that terrible trip, and now that my wife is under the same roof as me, you'd think I'd be more relaxed. Unfortunately, that is *not* the case.

I miss seeing her and Zo together. I miss watching them late at night while she nurses Zoey back to sleep. I miss watching her mix up bottles for her, or dancing around the kitchen singing obnoxious lullabies off key, just to calm our sleeping baby. I've never seen a better mother than her, and the fact that I haven't gotten to witness that lately, is eating me alive. I'd like to think that I'll be home soon, but I don't want to get my hopes up. I don't know if she believes me yet. It still hurts to think that she believed I slept with another woman, but at this point, I just need her back. I feel like a vital limb is missing from my body when I'm without her.

I close my eyes, hoping to fall asleep. The point is most likely moot, but my damn head is killing me from all the stress from the last day. As I start to doze off, my phone dings from the coffee table.

"Fuck." The only reason I check it is to make sure that it's not Lucy texting me about Zoey. It's my sister.

Claire: How's Av?
Me: I don't know. She's been locked in our room since we got home.
Claire: Just give her time. She'll come around.
Me: We'll see. I'll call you in the morning.
Claire: Alright. Let me know if you guys need anything. Love you big bro.

I throw my phone back on the table and sigh. It's taking all the restraint I have to keep from going to my wife. I want more than anything, to go in there and hold her close and never let her out of my sight again.

I jolt awake out of a restless sleep. *Screaming.* I hear screaming. What the hell is going on? I run to the bedroom and rattle the door, apparently thinking that'll cause the lock to budge.

"Av?" I shout, but get no response. She's crying, and I can't fucking get to her.

I sprint to the kitchen to get a butter knife to release the lock. I can't seem to get the damn thing open fast enough. I have no idea what's going on behind the closed door, but I know that I need to get to her.

As soon as the door opens, the sight before me nearly cuts me in half. Avery is sitting on the edge of the bed, holding her stomach as she's hunched over. I'm not sure if she's fully awake, so I decide against approaching her right away. I hear whimpering, and my heart nearly pounds out of my chest.

She finally settles back on the bed before she notices that I'm standing in the doorway.

"Ev?" she croaks out, and that's the last straw for me before I go to her. I can't stay away any longer. I need this woman as much as she needs me, and I'm done holding back. I'm done letting her push me away.

"I'm here." I crawl in next to her and carefully pull her to my chest, mindful of her bandaged-up nose and broken ribs. It fucking makes me insane seeing her like this. I inhale the intoxicating scent of lavender on her skin and hair. I started buying her the stuff when we started dating, and ever since, it's all that she's used. Say what you want, but as soon as she runs out of it, I go to the girly ass store and buy her more. It makes her happy, and the damn smell is amazing mixed with her natural scent.

"You okay?" I whisper into her hair before kissing the top of her head. She doesn't pull away from me. I'm not sure how long this moment will last, so I'm cherishing whatever I can get from her.

"I- I had a nightmare." I feel a tear hit my naked chest.

"Nobody is going to hurt you again. Not if I can help it." I rub my hand up and down her arm, trying to soothe her back to sleep.

"Thank you," she says shyly, and I hate that she feels she has to be that way with me.

Her tense body soon relaxes into mine, which in return makes me relax into the bed. It's been too long since I've slept beside her, but in this moment, it feels like no time has passed.

❧ 42 ❧

AVERY

When I wake, I notice that the other side of the bed looks like it was slept in. *It wasn't a dream.* When Evan brought me home yesterday, I locked myself in our room. I wasn't trying to be a bitch, I just haven't wanted to talk much about what happened to me. I promised myself that I'd talk to my husband and try to work things out with him, but now that he's here with me, I've done nothing but push him away again. I remember him holding me last night until I fell back asleep. I hadn't felt that safe in a long time.

I should probably get up to start my day. Evan wants to take me to see Zoey this morning. As much as I want to see my baby, I don't want to get my mom's hopes up. She'll assume we're back together, and she'll be throwing a party for us to celebrate.

Finally, deciding to get up, I carefully lift myself from the bed and go to the bathroom to relieve my bladder and then start the tub, adding some of my favorite bubble bath. My pain seems to be manageable today, but I still have to remember to take it easy. I tend to overdo it at times, and I really don't want to end up back in the hospital.

I strip out of my clothes and then un-Velcro my brace that wraps around my midsection. I stare at the bruises that mar my pale skin, and a rush of sadness hits me. I've felt so many emotions over the last couple days, but right now, I'm just trying to understand why someone did this to me. I don't think I'll feel better until we know who did this to me.

I carefully step into the tub and lower myself into the water. At first, the movement is painful, but once the warmth hits my body, I'm able to relax a bit. I lean my head against my bath pillow, now wondering how the hell I'm going to get out of this tub once I'm done. *Shit.* I didn't think this through very well.

My eyes fly open at the insistent pounding on the door. *What the hell?* Shit, I must have fallen asleep. The water is now cold, so I try to stand to grab for my towel, but immediately regret the movement.

"Oww!" I cry out as I hold my stomach. I'm shaking profusely while in pain. This is too much.

I'm scared to sit back in the tub because the movement will most likely only increase the pain. I'm mindful not to slip, but I continue to shiver as I know there's no way I can get to my towel. Not on my own at least.

"Av?" I hear Evan from the door, and I'm relieved yet suddenly self-conscious, standing here butt naked. I know I shouldn't feel that way in front of my husband, but he hasn't seen my battered body yet.

In the next instant, I'm being wrapped in a warm towel.

"What happened?" he whispers into my ear, "Did you hurt yourself?"

"I- I just wanted a bath and must have fallen asleep. When you knocked on the door, I tried getting up, but it hurt like hell." I'm ashamed at how careless I was.

I look up at his face, and I can tell he's worried. "If you're going to take a bath without me around, keep your phone near you so you can call for help. And damn it woman, don't fall asleep in the bathtub." He sighs.

"Can you help me out?"

"Yeah, come on." He grabs my hand as I lift my legs out of the tub and then walks me out of the bathroom, careful to make sure I don't slip on the wet floor.

He walks me to the bed and helps me sit. "Stay put, I'll grab your brace for you." He turns back to the bathroom, and I feel the familiar sting behind my eyes, caused from the tears that are fighting to get out. I want him back so damn much, but I don't know if he still wants me. I don't notice he's back in the room until he speaks again, "Av, what's wrong? You hurt still?" He kneels in front of me, between my legs as he runs a hand through my hair.

I wipe at my wet face. Crying makes my broken nose burn. I feel like a freaking mess.

"No. I'm okay," I rasp out, and I can tell he's not buying my bullshit, but thankfully drops it. "Let me get dressed, and we'll go see Zo."

"Yeah, okay." He nods and then stands, but before he reaches the door turns to me again. "Do you need help getting dressed?" I can tell he's concerned, yet at the same time, worried about what my reaction will be.

"I'll be fine. Just give me a few minutes, and I'll be out."

He doesn't say anything else before he leaves the room.

"HOW YOU FEELIN', baby girl?" my dad asks as he gently hugs me, knowing that I'm still in pain.

"I'm fine, Daddy." I look up at him.

"You don't have to be fine all the time, you know? Why don't you sit down, and I'll go make you some coffee?"

I nod, knowing that arguing with him is pointless. If my dad wants to take care of me, he's going to.

We just arrived at my parents' house, and when my mom said that Zoey was sleeping, Evan went to check on her. I feel like I've been completely selfish in keeping her from him. Not that I ever told him he couldn't see her, but it's not the same as being together all the time as a family. I don't know how to make this right.

"Here you go. Just like you always take it." Dad hands me the steaming mug of sugary goodness. I blow on it before taking a small sip.

"Thanks." I give him a half smile. "And thanks for keeping Zo for us."

"You know that we'd do anything for you and that little princess. We're just glad you're alright. You gave us quite a scare. I don't know what I would have done if you would have been hurt more seriously." I never see this side of him. It cuts my heart in two, knowing that I did this to him. Okay, I know that technically the attack wasn't my fault, but I hate knowing that he's hurting because of me.

"I promise, I'm fine." I reach my hand across the couch to give his a tight squeeze. "Evan is working with the police, but I promise, the pain isn't that bad."

"There's Momma." I hear Evan and look up to see him carrying our beautiful girl.

"Hi baby!" I get a big smile from her, and I suddenly feel a lot better. I hate being away from her, much less for two nights. "Here, I'll take her." I try standing, but the pain in my ribs is too intense, and I'm halted in my movement.

"She's super wiggly right now. I don't know if that's a good idea."

"Well, at least sit next to me with her so I can see her." He complies and sits by me. I'm excited to see my daughter, but having him this close to me again, without touching him, is driving me crazy.

We're left in the living room alone, and spend the next forty-five minutes as a family reading to Zoey and playing with her toys. Evan and I don't talk a lot besides interacting with our daughter, but I'm done pushing him away. I need this man, and I need to figure out how to rebuild our marriage.

❧ 43 ❧

AVERY

"You go get ready for bed, and I'll get Zoey settled for the night," Evan says as we walk through the garage door. We ended up spending the rest of the day visiting with my parents.

"Okay." I kiss Zoey on top the head and then head toward our room and strip out of my clothes. I still can't move fast, so I take my time, trying to avoid causing myself any more pain. Tonight, I really don't feel like seeing my bruises again, so I decided not to step foot inside the bathroom until I'm dressed. I pull my yoga pants and racerback tank top over my head, sans a bra. Trying to get the damn thing on earlier hurt like hell. I'm kind of surprised that Evan didn't offer to come in to help me, but I think he wanted to give me a bit of space. I feel like we've jumped over a hurdle today, but he knows how bullheaded I am. I really need to work on that.

After I'm dressed, I grab my Kindle off the nightstand and then walk to Zoey's room.

"She's already asleep?" I whisper to Evan as he walks out of the nursery.

He gives me a small smile. "Yeah, she must have been exhausted. I'm glad to have her home though."

I'm glad too. Evan and my dad insisted that Evan continue to stay with me until I'm better, especially since I wanted Zoey home with me. I was too tired to put up a fight, but I have to admit I love having us all under the same roof again.

"Me too." I carefully settle into the couch and see Evan out of the corner of my eye, watching to make sure I'm alright. "I think I'm just going to lay here and read a bit. I'm pretty tired."

"Okay. You may have overdone it today. You want me to make you some coffee?" A small smile tugs at my lips. This man and his sweet gestures are about to bring me to my knees.

"Sure."

"I'll be right back." He kisses me on the cheek, and the butterflies take flight in my stomach. His lips linger for a few seconds, and then he stands to leave the room.

Damn, I've missed him so much.

I open my Kindle up to a book I bought the other day that I haven't gotten to start yet. Claire got me hooked on romance books. She published her first book right before her and Ryke got married. Typically, they make me feel better on days I'm feeling like a hot mess, but lately, my life is feeling more and more like the characters I read about. This is real life though. They always get their happily ever after. Will I?

I'm only three pages in when I see Evan carrying my mug of coffee toward me.

"Reading anything good?" he asks as he sets the mug on the coffee table and then lifts my feet so he can sit under them. He starts mindlessly massaging my feet, and I don't want him to stop.

I try to pull myself up to a sitting position, but a bolt of pain shoots through my ribs.

I must gasp louder than I think because Evan is up in the next second helping me.

"You okay?" He props a pillow behind my back and then brushes my hair away from my eyes. I wish so bad right now that I wasn't feeling so shitty. His masculine woodsy smell permeates through the air. I'd be half tempted to take him to our bedroom and have my way with him, if I wasn't feeling like shit. We'll never work through our issues if we try to solve everything with sex. Although, I can't say I'd turn him down.

"Yeah." I lean my head back, trying to ward off the tears. I feel like such an emotional mess right now. Between the pain and being so close to my husband after what seems like forever.

"Here, why don't you take a drink?" He lifts the hot drink to my lips, and I blow on it before taking a sip.

"Thanks," I whisper up at him.

"You're welcome." I can hear the emotion in his voice, and it's ripping me apart.

After I take another drink, he takes the mug from me and sets it on the table.

"You don't have to be alright all the time. You know that?" He strokes at my hair.

I squeeze my eyes shut and then stare up into his handsome brown eyes.

"My dad said the same thing today."

"He's a smart man." He squats next to me and grabs my hand. "Av, I'm so sorry about what happened the other night. I wish more than anything that I could take your pain away and make it all better for you." I can hear the sincerity in his voice.

I finally stop holding back, and the tears flow freely down my face.

"Let it out, Av. You've been through a lot." He holds me the best he can while I'm lying awkwardly on the couch and he's crouched next to me on the floor. "I'm so, so sorry." He coos into my ear, and it makes me feel somewhat better.

The nightmares the last two nights were unbearable. I'm scared to close my eyes again tonight. I know I'm supposed to be resting, but it's the last thing I want to do.

"Thanks, Ev," I say when the tears finally start to let up. He wipes at my cheek.

"You have nothing to thank me for. I'm always here." Those simple words lift the heavy weight that's been pulling me down. I was already starting to feel like we were getting somewhere earlier in the day, but I needed to hear that from him. I want to believe him. That he really does always want to take care of me, but what if the damage is too severe?

I can't find the words to say, so I respond with a light smile. I swear I'm more hormonal now than I was during my entire pregnancy.

"Want me to help you to the bed? I'll stay out here again." I think he's trying to make me feel better, but the pain is back in my chest. I don't want him to leave me, but I'm scared to tell him that.

"Actually, I thought maybe we could find something to

watch on Netflix. Unless you're tired." It's a good excuse to spend more time with him, but also prolongs the inevitable. I know it's only been a couple days, but I worry that this nightmare will never get better.

"Yeah, that sounds good. You want me to get you anything to eat before we start it up?"

"I'm okay. I ate enough to feed an army at Mom and Dad's today."

He throws his head back in laughter. "Good point. If she ever stops feeding us, I'm protesting."

I love seeing his playful side. I've missed seeing him like this.

"Do you want me to help you into your recliner so you're more comfortable?" He eyes me with concern, and I could get lost in the sea of chocolate that is staring back at me.

"Yeah, that's a good idea."

He puts one arm behind me and the other under my legs and carefully lifts me from the couch.

"Oww." I take a quick breath and close my eyes, trying to ward off the pain.

"Did I hurt you?" I open my eyes at his question and shake my head.

"No. It just hurts anyway. You didn't do anything wrong."

He carries me to my chair, and after he sets me down, he pulls the lever to lift my feet off the ground. This is much better than laying on the too-soft couch.

"Better?" he asks as he reclines in the twin seat next to me. We bought these a few years back and always use them when we watch movies. We could just buy a couch that reclines, but we just moved them right next to each other so we can be close.

"Yeah." I turn and smile at him sleepily. I can feel my pain meds starting to kick in and wonder how long I'll actually be able to stay awake to watch a movie. "You can choose something."

He scrolls through Netflix, and I laugh when I see what he settles on.

"Really?" I raise my eyebrows at him. "You're going to seriously sit here and watch *The Wedding Date* with me?" He despises chick flicks, almost as much as I can't stand the weird sci-fi shit he always wants to watch.

He reaches over and pushes a loose strand of hair behind my ear.

"If I get to see that beautiful smile light up your face, I'd watch fucking *Twilight* with you."

Not letting me respond, he turns the movie on. Just as I expected, I'm asleep before the credits are over.

44

EVAN

The coffee maker beeps at me, indicating the pot is finished brewing. The smells of bacon, toast, and freshly ground coffee fill my nostrils. It smells like home. *This is my home.* Not because it's the four walls we decided to live in to start our family. No, because it's where my beautiful wife and daughter are.

I plate our food before I hear little cries coming from Zoey's room. It's not her angry cry. No, it's her attention-seeking cry that she just started in the last month. It makes me laugh, although I'm sure we won't think it's cute when she's older trying to get away with that shit. Good thing she's my little princess.

I wipe my hands on a towel before making my way to her.

"Hey, princess." I look down at our girl, and she's swinging her arms in the air.

I lift Zoey out of the crib, and she reaches for the scruff on my face. I playfully try to bite her finger that she shoves in my mouth. I never realized how much I wanted to be a father until she was born.

She swats at my face, and I grab her hand and kiss it.

"Don't hit your daddy."

After Avery fell asleep last night, I carried her to our bed and then slept out on the couch. I wanted to crawl under the sheets with her so badly, but I wasn't sure if she wanted that. Thankfully, she didn't wake again with a nightmare. I know better than to think that they're gone for good. I just want to make sure I'm by her side when the next one wakes her.

"There's Momma," I say as we walk into our bedroom. My girl is propped up against the headboard, reading on her Kindle. If it makes her happy, then I'll buy her all the fucking books in the world.

"Hi, baby," Avery says as she rubs Zoey's head. "Here, I'll take her." She reaches her arms out to take her from me. I feel like I'm starting to get my wife back one piece at a time, so this is probably not the time to act like an alpha asshole. "Ev, I promise I'll be careful." She obviously can read the reluctance on my face.

"If you're sure." I set Zoey on her lap and then kiss the top of Avery's head. "You want some breakfast? I made eggs, bacon, toast, and coffee."

Her face lights up. "I'd love some. Can you bring me my medicine first though off the bathroom counter?"

"Sure." I grab her medicine and a glass of water from the kitchen and then head back to our room.

"You feeling okay?" I hand her the tablet and water.

"Yeah, actually much better. I just want to make sure I keep the pain under control." I nod at her and can't help but stare at the beautiful woman in front of me, holding our daughter. The product of our love. The child we wanted for years and couldn't have, but when we were ready to give up, we were finally lucky enough to have this little girl. "I think I just need to take it easy today."

I don't tell her that I agree but instead just nod my head. I'm sure she can tell that I'm holding back. When it comes to this woman, I go fucking crazy worrying about her.

"Do you want me to bring your food in here?"

"No, I think it would be good for me to get up for a bit. It makes me sorer if I sit for too long."

"Okay, let me go put Zoey in the other room, and then I'll help you up."

After setting Zoey in her swing, I carefully help Avery off the bed.

"You alright?" I look down at her, worried I may have hurt her again like I did last night.

"Yeah, I'm fine." She smiles up at me. "I can walk now."

Once we're in the kitchen, she settles into a chair at the table.

I pour her a cup of coffee and put her food in front of her. I've missed this. Before, I had just thought about how I wanted to be back here with her and Zoey, but I've also missed the small things we do together.

"Mmm." She groans around a fork full of eggs, and my shorts suddenly grow fucking tight. She has no idea how erotic she is being right now.

I want so badly to say something to her about it, or just take her to our room and have my way with her, but that won't be happening today. Anyway, the next time I make love to her, I want to know that I'm getting her back for good. My damn heart can't take any more rejection.

"Um…" I start, and now, I'm not sure if this is going to piss her off, so I pause.

She takes a sip from her mug. "What is it?"

"Claire is going to come hang out with you and Zo for a bit this afternoon."

"Where do you have to go?"

I sigh. "I'm going down to the police station to talk to Anthony some more."

She nods as she takes a sip of her coffee. "Yeah, okay. Have you heard anything yet?"

"No, not yet." I take a bite of my eggs. "There were cameras in the parking lot, but whoever did this to you seemed to have known where they all were."

I see the fear in her eyes, so I squeeze her hand. "Av, I promise you, I will never let someone hurt you or our daughter again."

She shakes her head. "You can't promise that, Evan." She stands from the table to take her dishes to the sink, and I follow behind her.

I gently run my hands through her hair, not wanting to cause more pain from her injuries. "I know I can't promise that, but you better believe that I'm going to work my ass off to protect you and our daughter. Do you understand me?"

She looks up at me with watery eyes. I decide there's no better time than now to bite the bullet. I want to figure out who the hell did this to my wife, and then I just want to move on with our lives. Put this all behind us.

"I didn't cheat on you, Av," I say gently as I look down at her.

"I know," she says as tears start to fall.

I'm sure she can see the shock on my face. "You do?"

She sighs and then looks away from me. "I shouldn't have doubted you in the first place, but Claire and Sierra both talked some sense into me."

I give her a small smile. "You know I'd never even dream of doing something like that to you, right?"

She puts her head in her hands, and I hear a sob escape her.

"Av, it must have looked really bad, so I can't really be upset." I throw my head back. "Mallory came to my room and tried to be inappropriate, and when she wouldn't leave, I did. That's why she answered both the phones, because I got another room and I left my phone in there."

"I know, and I'm so sorry," she whispers. "I should have let you explain instead of jumping to conclusions."

"You don't need to apologize, okay? I just need you back."

"Okay, you've got me back." She sighs into my chest, inhaling my scent. "I hate that bitch for doing this to us."

I chuckle and then kiss her forehead. "Me too." I stroke at her messy hair. "I'm so sorry for not listening to you about her. I'm such an idiot."

She shakes her head. "No, you're a guy, and guys don't always notice how sneaky and underhanded some women can be."

"You're beautiful, you know that?"

She rolls her eyes. "I just woke up, and this thing..." She points to her nose, "makes me look like a fucking walrus," she mumbles.

"You're the most adorable walrus I've ever seen," I say as I kiss her neck, and she swats at my chest.

In the next second, her playful side is gone, and she looks lost in thought, which has me a little worried.

"What's wrong?"

"The night of the attack, I had wanted to come see you, but then ended up having to work late."

I'm sure I have a shocked look on my face, but I wasn't expecting that.

"What? You wanted to see me?" She hasn't once told me that she wanted to see or talk to me since we split up. This feels like fucking Christmas.

"Yeah." She puts her head down in embarrassment, so I lift her chin so she has to look at me.

"I'm glad." I lean down, and for the first time in weeks, I kiss my wife. I kiss her like my life depends on it.

When I finally pull back from her, I look into her clover eyes. "Please tell me to come home."

"Come home, Ev." She collapses into my arms, and I catch her as I carefully slide us both down to the floor.

All the emotions from the last several weeks, have finally caught up to me. Also, it feels good to cry with her after being apart for so long. I've missed this woman so damn much.

"You mean it?" I ask as I search her eyes for any doubt I might find.

"Yes. We need you here with us."

"Thank fuck."

In the next instant, I'm devouring her mouth like a starving man. I'd love to take her to bed right now and spend the next week making love to her, but I know that can't happen until she's healed.

45

EVAN

"Hello?" I answer my phone after the second ring, not bothering to see who's calling at this God-awful time of day.

I mindlessly stroke Avery's hair as she leans over my chest to look at the clock. My girl is *not* a morning person.

"Evan, it's Anthony."

I feel her tense, and it's obvious she can hear him.

"Yeah, what's up?" I quickly kiss the side of her face and then get out of bed. I should probably not have this conversation around her. I have no idea what he's about to tell me.

I grab my pants and then make my way out to the front porch. As soon as the front door slams shut behind me, I hear him sigh.

"I need you to come down to the station."

The thought that they may have a lead on Avery's attacker makes the hair stand up on the back of my neck. I spent all afternoon at the station yesterday, and last I heard, they still didn't know anything.

"What's going on?"

He doesn't respond right away, which has me more on edge. "Remember my buddy, Officer Caden Harris?"

I do remember him. He's met us at Ryke's a few times for a beer. Seemed like a nice enough guy, but I don't know where the hell he's going with this.

"Yes…." I say hesitantly.

"Well," he pauses, and I hear shuffling of papers in the background. "He pulled a woman over late last night for speeding, but she had a picture of you and a baby, I'm assuming Zoey, on her dashboard."

The thought gives me a sinking feeling in my gut. Who the hell would have a picture of me and my daughter? In their car, nonetheless.

"What the fuck?" I bark out.

"Dude, calm down. Just get down here so Caden can talk to you, alright?"

"Yeah, alright. You think this has to do with Avery's attack?"

"We don't know, but we're trying to figure that out."

I hang up and then throw my head back in frustration. This is so fucking messed up, and I know I can't tell Avery what Anthony just told me, because she'll freak the hell out. Not that I could really blame her.

I don't feel comfortable leaving her and Zoey home alone, so I send my sister a quick text asking her to invite Avery for breakfast. Claire is nosey, but doesn't ask questions. She knows we're trying to get to the bottom of this.

I walk back into the house, and she's feeding Zoey, but thankfully doesn't ask questions. I don't know what I would say to her right now anyway.

"Claire is coming to get me and Zo in an hour to go to breakfast."

I smile at her and then kiss the top of her head. "Sounds good."

She gives me a small smile, the concern obvious in her eyes. "Everything okay?"

I pull away from her and run a hand through my hair and sigh. "It will be. Let me handle it, alright?"

She nods, but I can tell she doesn't like my response.

"Go have fun with Claire, and then we'll order Chinese tonight. Sound good?"

She relaxes into the rocking chair. "Yeah."

AN HOUR LATER, I'm walking into the PD, ready to find out what the hell is going on. I didn't leave home until I knew that my wife and daughter weren't alone. The protective asshole that I am, I text Ryke asking him to go with the girls. I just need to know that they're safe until we find out who the hell hurt her.

"Hey, man." Anthony greets me when I walk into the building.

I shake his hand. "Hey, thanks for calling."

He nods and then leads me back to his cubicle where Officer Harris is waiting for us.

"Evan." He stands from his seat and shakes my hand.

"Hey, Anthony said you may have a lead on my wife's attack?" I cringe inside, realizing I'm about to find out who hurt her, but not knowing has been killing me inside.

He sits back down and points to the chair across from him as Anthony takes the seat behind his desk.

He leans his elbows on his knees. "Do you know a Mallory Parker?"

What the actual fuck? I immediately see red. Did she fucking do this to Avery?

"Did- did she do this?" I clear my throat.

"How do you know her?" Caden asks.

I don't answer right away, so Anthony chimes in. "She was his assistant and the one who split him and Avery up. She made her think that they slept together."

Caden raises his eyebrows at me. "Seriously?"

I grab the back of my neck, desperately needing to punch something. I'm not one for hitting women, but let's just say Mallory is damn lucky she's not within my reach.

"How the fuck did she get a picture of me and my daughter?"

He stands from his chair. "I don't know, but we need to get to the bottom of this. Me and Anthony are going to go to her house and question her."

I answer with a nod. I know they won't let me, but I want to go with them. Although, it's probably best I don't. I just got my wife back; I don't want to land my own ass in jail.

Anthony types away on his laptop and then spins it toward me.

"This her?" On the screen is what appears to be Mallory's Facebook profile picture.

"That's her."

Caden moves closer to look at it. "Yep, that's who I pulled over yesterday."

"God damn it." I grip at my hair in frustration.

THAT NIGHT, my phone vibrates in my pocket while we're at dinner at Claire and Ryke's. I glance at the screen and see that it's Anthony. I've been waiting for his call all day, and I know I've been acting like an ass while being on pins and needles until I know what the hell is going on.

I stand from the table, and Avery gives me a questioning look, but I ignore it while I walk out of the room. I haven't told her that Mallory is a prime suspect of her attack yet. I wanted to know for sure.

"What'd you find out?" I ask in way of answering as I walk outside. Nobody else needs to hear this conversation.

I hear him sigh heavily. "Her fingerprints matched the ones found on Avery's car after the attack."

I suddenly have a sick feeling in my stomach, and I think I may need to throw up.

"Evan, you there?" Anthony asks when I don't respond.

"Yeah. I'm here."

"We found her fingerprints, but she also admitted to attacking her. We now have her in custody."

I drop my phone on the sidewalk and immediately evacuate the contents of my stomach in one of the bushes.

This is my fucking fault. She attacked my wife because I got her fired for the shit she pulled in Dallas.

I hear Anthony on the other line, calling my name, but I can't bear to hear another word about this.

"Ev?" I hear Avery call out as she runs down the driveway. "What's wrong?"

Once I'm confident that I won't puke again, I stand back up and then wipe my mouth with the back of my hand.

"It was Mallory," I rasp out. She gives me a confused look, but then I can tell when she understands what I'm talking about.

"She attacked me?" I see the tears in her eyes, and I want nothing more than to keep her locked away, where I know she'll be safe. I don't care how much of an ass that makes me. I didn't protect her before, and now, she's suffered because of it.

I can't speak, so I answer with a nod.

Her face goes pale, and in the next moment, her legs give out, but I quickly catch her.

"Let's get you inside," I lift her into my arms.

As soon as we walk inside, I carry her to the guest bedroom I had been staying in. I lay her on the bed and let her weep into my chest.

Finally, after what feels like hours, she stares up at me, her tears starting to dry on her face.

I tuck a stray hair behind her ear.

"I'm so sorry, Av. This is all my fault." I just got my wife back, and now, we have to face all this shit.

She pulls out of my arms. "Evan Porter, don't you dare blame yourself. You hear me? This is not your fault."

I squeeze her into my chest, not wanting to ever let her go. "Why are you so good to me?"

She looks up at me. "Because I love you."

I smile down at her. "I love you, too." I take her into a kiss.

"Av, we're going to get through this together." She nods. "I swear to you, I'll never let another person lay a hand on you again."

"Okay."

"Okay?" I ask her, wanting to make sure she believes me.

"Yeah." She nods. "Let's go get Zo and go home."

I grab her face and take her mouth into mine, never wanting to be away from this woman again.

❧ 46 ❧

AVERY

It's been two months since Evan came back home, and I can honestly say, they have been the best two months of my life. I'm still healing from the attack, so we haven't gotten to be physical, besides kissing and groping, but the man has made me so happy.

We are still waiting for Mallory's trial, but it's a relief to know she's behind bars.

I decided not to go back to work at Kinsley. I knew that Evan didn't want me to either, but he let me decide this on my own. After the assault, I didn't feel safe, but also, I want to spend all the time I can with Zoey while she's young. In a few months, I'm going to start doing some private designing from home, but I've already decided that I'll only take on one or two clients at a time.

"Knock, knock," Evan says from the bathroom door before lifting me into his arms. "You ready to go, birthday girl?" He kisses along my neck, and I try swatting him away, but he doesn't let up.

"Ev!" I giggle. "You're going to mess my hair up."

He looks at me through the mirror and smirks. "We could just stay home, and I can mess your hair up all night."

"No way. I worked my ass off to look this good." I wink at him before passing him to grab my earrings from my jewelry box.

He huffs in exaggeration.

"Fine." He walks past me and swats my ass. "Hurry up then."

I roll my eye at his dramatics. Tonight, I'm wearing my auburn hair up in a chignon, in hopes that I won't die from the heat. I've always had long hair, but this time of year it stays up most of the time, because I can't stand it sticking to my neck. It's so damn hot out.

The dress I'm wearing is an emerald green halter-top. It makes my boobs look amazing. Evan bought it for me with a matching bra and panties. I'm hoping the panties get torn to shit tonight. Cut me a break. I'm freaking horny. I've been under the same roof as my husband for eight weeks and haven't gotten to do much. I had a doctor's appointment yesterday, and he agreed to me not wearing the obnoxious brace any longer. My ribs don't hurt anymore, so he said that as long as I'm careful I can get back to regular activity. And well, sex is definitely a regular activity around here.

I grab my sexy strappy heels and make my way out to the kitchen.

"Did Zo do okay when you dropped her off with Claire?" I grab a bottle of water out of the fridge. This is the first time I've been left alone in the last two months, but I thought it would be a good idea to do a small trial run while Zo wasn't here. I handled it a lot better than I thought I would.

"Yeah, she was already playing with Aria when I left." He kisses me on the cheek. "Tonight, I want to practice for number two."

I roll my eyes at him. I thought that joking around like this would upset me, but it really doesn't. After he moved back home, we decided that we aren't going to try for another baby. If it happens, it happens, but the heartbreak before having Zoey was terrible and neither of us want to go through that again. But we still would like to have more children, even if not biologically.

Next week, we start foster care classes. Our end goal is to eventually adopt. We've met a few other families who have successfully adopted a child, and we know that heartache can also rear its ugly head with adopting, but we've both come to realize that we can face anything as long as we have each other.

"How do you know I want to practice?" I wiggle my eyebrows at him, and he knows I'm full of shit.

"Because I know my wife, and I know that she's a little sex fiend." He wraps his arms around me from behind as he nibbles at my neck. His hands find their way to my boobs, and I halt his movements.

"Ev, stop." Now I'm panting.

He pulls away from me, and I moan in frustration.

"What?" He raises his eyebrows at me. "You told me to stop."

"What time is our reservation?"

"We don't have one." *Just the words I wanted to hear.*

"Good." In the next instant, my dress is flying through

the air, and I'm now standing before my husband in only my bra, panties, and heels.

"Holy. Fuck," Evan says as he looks at me like he wants to have *me* for dinner.

"Why are you looking at me like that?"

He wastes no time in his walk toward me, and then my lips are being covered by his. This kiss is all teeth and tongue and speaks of how hungry he is for me.

I pull away from him. "Mr. Porter, you have got to lose the clothes."

He smirks at me. "Yes, ma'am." He slowly drags his dress pants down his legs and is now in front of me in nothing but his shirt and red boxers. He unbuttons his shirt and slides it down his arms. Before he can get to his boxers, I take it upon myself to help him, and I go to the floor with them.

I look up at him, and he smiles down at me.

"What are you doing?" He croaks out, and I can tell I'm affecting him. I've pleasured him a few times like this over the last few weeks, but tonight, I plan on taking things much further. I'm hoping he'll just cancel whatever plans he had for us and keep me locked up in our room all night.

I stroke his long shaft and then slowly take the tip into my mouth, moaning around it as I go.

"Oh, fuck." He throws his head back. "Right there." He grabs me by the hair and pumps into my mouth. I can taste his pre-cum, and I'm getting more turned on by the damn minute. I can feel the wetness pool between my legs, and I don't know how long I can wait for him to be inside of me.

"I should be giving you a gift today for your birthday."

I release him from my mouth.

"You can if you want." I wink at him and then take him back into my mouth. In the next second, I'm being lifted into the air, and then I'm on top of the counter.

I giggle as he pulls at the sides of my panties, and just as I had hoped, rips them from my body.

"Hey! I liked those!" I jokingly say, but I'm really about to come undone at any minute.

"I'll buy you more just like them."

Once my panties are on the floor, he spreads my legs and then wastes no time in devouring my core.

"Ahh!" I scream, and it's going to be a damn miracle if I last long. It has been way too long. I have a feeling that nothing about this night is going to be slow or sweet. Thank fuck though, I'm too turned on for that.

He lightly pushes on my stomach, directing me to lay back on the counter as his tongue continues to move in and out of me. He uses his finger to rub my clit, and that's all it takes to cause me to start seeing fireworks behind my eyelids.

"Ev!" I holler, and I'm pretty sure our neighbors just heard me, but I'm too damned lost in his touch to care.

Once I'm finally able to open my eyes after the best orgasm I've ever had, he lifts me off the counter, into his arms.

No words are spoken as he kisses along my neck and then my mouth again.

When we make it to our room, he lays me on the bed and crawls on top of me.

"I'm going to worship this body all night long," he whispers into my hair.

"Please do," I moan as I run my hands through his hair.

The scruff from his beard is rubbing against my chest, and the sensation is making me even wetter.

"Are you ready for me, Av?" He wraps his lips around one of my nipples as he twists the other one between his fingers.

"God, yes!" That's all the invitation he needs before he's slamming into me.

He pulls away from my nipple and gives me a concerned look.

"You okay?"

I nod. "Yes. Please don't stop."

He lifts himself up and pulls my legs over his shoulders so he's able to drive into me further. I didn't realize how much I missed sex until this moment. This man knows exactly how to set my body on fire.

He continues thrusting in and out and then rubs at me with his finger.

"Come for me, Av." He pumps one last time before I'm screaming in ecstasy.

He releases my legs and then soon finds his own release. I feel him filling me, and I wish that we could stay like this forever.

Once we both catch our breath, he rolls over and then pulls me into his side.

"I fucking love you, Avery Porter." He kisses the top of my head.

"And I fucking love you, too, Evan Porter."

"I'm never letting you go again."

I smile up at him and then kiss his cheek. "Good, because I'm never letting you go again either."

EPILOGUE

AVERY

"Happy birthday, princess," Evan says to Zoey as he bends down to kiss the top of her crown-covered head.

"Daddy! You're gonna mess up my pretty hair!" our daughter yells at him, and it has us both chuckling.

Today is her fourth birthday. I don't know where the time has gone, but I've loved watching her turn into the beautiful girl she is. Evan always thought she looked like me when she was a baby, but today, she looks just like her daddy with dark brown pigtails in her hair.

"Well, I wouldn't want to mess your pretty hair up. I'm so sorry, princess." He leaves Zoey and then pulls me into his arms. "How is she four already?"

I sigh. "I have no idea." I look up at my handsome husband and smile at him.

Ever since we got back together a few years ago, we have both worked hard to keep our marriage exactly the way we want it. It hasn't always been easy, but at the end of each day, it's been worth it. I've never loved anyone as much as I love this man and our three daughters. *Yes, I said three.*

A year and a half ago, the adoption of our twin six-year-old daughters, Lily and Jade, was finalized. Soon after we finished taking our foster care course, we were able to bring the two little blondes into our home. They were three when we got them, so we had our hands full, but we wouldn't have wanted it any other way. They had been in the system since they were born, but hadn't yet found a family who was able to adopt them together. I would never dream of separating the little beauties. Those two girls have taught me so much over the last few years. I couldn't love them more, even if they were my biological children.

Evan and Malcom ended up buying Howser & Bowman out from Flynn. They were already one of the top firms in Phoenix, but the two of them have made it even better since taking over. I'm damn proud of my man and what he's accomplished over the years.

"Mommy and Daddy, can I open my presents now?" Zo interrupts us.

"Of course. Let's gather everyone into the living room."

I go in search of all the other kids who are playing in the twins' room. Most of the other kids here are younger than them, so they all think their toys are "cool."

"Hey girls, Zo's going to open her gifts. Can you help me get everyone out to the other room?"

Lily walks up to me and wraps her tiny arms around me. "Sure, Momma. We're the big kids, so we'll take charge."

I smirk down at her as I squeeze her in return.

"Thanks, Lil." I kiss the top of her head. She's been my little love bug since both girls came to live with us. Jade was a little more hesitant, but Lily latched onto me right away, as if she'd known me since birth. Thankfully, it didn't take much time for her sister to come around, but she is definitely a Daddy's girl.

It only takes Zo about fifteen minutes to open all her gifts because the girl wastes no time when she wants something. We then cut into her cake and, of course, all the kiddos are covered in chocolate by the time they're done eating.

Before having Zoey, this would have bothered me, but now, I can't imagine my life being less than chaotic.

Everyone important to us is here, besides Sierra and her boys. We've stayed in touch these last few years and have even taken all the girls out to see them during school breaks. It's fun having all our children around the same age.

Once everyone is out the door and we have three little girls in sugar comas, I go to our bedroom to get something I've been wanting to show Evan all day.

"What are you doing?" Evan asks as I take the seat next to him on the couch, butterflies swarming through my stomach.

"Uh… here." I thrust the bag at him, before chickening out.

"What's this?" he asks as he looks at the small gold gift bag. I'm hoping he's excited about this.

"Just look." My knee bounces in nervousness while impatiently waiting for him to pull the tissue paper out, and then I see him stare into the bag at the black and white picture.

After what feels like hours, he gives me his big handsome smile.

"Holy shit." He jumps off the couch, and in the next second, I'm in his arms. "You're pregnant?" he croaks out.

I never imagined him being this emotional, but it makes sense after all the struggles we had to get pregnant with Zo. We had decided that we weren't going to try again, but we hadn't exactly been careful either.

"Yeah." I smile up at him. "Are you happy?" I know he is by his expression, but I ask anyway.

"Am I happy? I'm fucking ecstatic." He kisses me like his life depends on it but then pulls away. "I can't believe we're going to have four kids."

"There's something else."

He pulls away from me. "Are we having twins?" He smirks, and it has me laughing.

"No, there's only one in there, but look under the sonogram."

He sits back on the couch and pulls the picture out, looking at our little peanut. He smiles at me in awe and then looks back in the bag and pulls the little pink booties out.

"We're having another girl?" The emotion on his face brings me to tears. He's such a good daddy to the three girls we already have. I can't wait to see him with this baby.

I nod. "Surprise!" I rub at my still small stomach.

"But I don't understand. If you just found out, how do you already know we're having a girl?"

"Because of my age, they did noninvasive prenatal testing, and they were able to reveal the gender as well. I hope you don't mind that I found out without you."

He shakes his head. "No, I don't mind. I'm just so fucking happy. But damn. Now I'm going to have to buy another gun."

I chuckle. "I think we're safe for a few years."

He pulls me into another hug and then kisses me like he never has before. This man is the best thing that's ever happened to me. Our marriage hasn't always been easy, but once we learned that our love was too important to give up on, we were renewed.

ALSO BY S.E. ROBERTS

VOYAGES OF THE HEART (LONDON) ANTHOLOGY

Love Refined

THE UNEXPECTED SERIES

Revived

Renewed

Reawakened (coming soon)

ACKNOWLEDGMENTS

With the love and support of so many people, Evan and Avery's story became exactly how I had hoped! When I wrote Revived, I never planned on making it into a series, but now, these characters have all come alive in my head. It's absolutely terrifying putting your work out there for the world, but with so many amazing people by my side, it has been better than I ever could have imagined.

As always, thank you to my husband, children, family, and best friend, Amanda, who have rooted for me since the beginning. Your love and support mean the world.

Jessica Ames, thank you so much for everything you do and for your daily encouragement. You're an incredible author, and an even more amazing friend. Love you! MA Foster, thank you for all you've taught me along the way and for taking me under your wing from the start.

I can't forget my WONDERFUL beta readers! Cindy Pippins, Andrea Galante, and Jessy Dulaney. Thank you all for helping make this book what it is today. Andrea, after you read Revived, you suggested I give Evan and Avery a story. So, thanks to you, Renewed happened!

Thank you to all my Rockin' Romancers for making me smile every day and loving my words.

Debra and Stracey: Your love for my books means everything to me. Every single other person who has spread the word about my books... you ALL are much appreciated!! Sharon, thank you for all your help and for being a sweet friend!

Last, but certainly not least, YOU the reader! Thanks for taking a chance on this new author. Without you, none of this would be possible.

ABOUT THE AUTHOR

S.E. Roberts was born and raised in the cornfields of Central Illinois, but now lives in sunny Arizona with her husband, two children, and her rescue cat, Stanley. When she isn't spending time with her family, she enjoys writing steamy romance, reading, and sipping on iced vanilla coffees. She continues to dream up her characters with the assistance of rocky road ice cream.

facebook.com/serobertsromance

twitter.com/authorSEroberts

instagram.com/authorseroberts